ALLEN COUNTY PUBLIC LIBRARY

3 1833 02   Y0-ACF-295

Fiction
Jackson, Dave.
Lost river conspiracy

RIVER CONSPIRACY

LOST RIVER CONSPIRACY

DAVE JACKSON

Good Books

Intercourse, PA 17534

Cover design and illustration by Cheryl Benner
Design by Dawn J. Ranck

LOST RIVER CONSPIRACY
Copyright © 1995 by Dave Jackson

Good Books, Intercourse, PA 17534
International Standard Book Number: 1-56148-183-1
Library of Congress Catalog Card Number: 95-31797

All rights reserved. Printed in the United States of America.
No part of this book may be reproduced in any manner,
except for brief quotations in critical articles or reviews,
without permission.

Library of Congress Cataloging-in-Publication Data
Jackson, Dave.
    Lost river conspiracy / Dave Jackson.
        p. cm.
    Summary: Captured by a young woman's beauty and strength and
incensed by her father's calloused intentions, Abe inserts himself into
a conflict involving the Modoc Indians.
    ISBN: 1-56148-183-1 (paperback)
    1. Frontier and pioneer life--West (U.S.)--Fiction. 2. Modoc Indians--
Wars, 1873--Fiction. [1. Frontier and pioneer life--West (U.S.)--Fiction.
2. Modoc Indians--Wars, 1873--Fiction.]
    I. Title
PS3560.A2128L67 1995
813'.54--dc20

Allen County Public Library
900 Webster Street
PO Box 2270
Fort Wayne, IN 46801-2270

95-31797
CIP
AC

To Julian, my son—a man of peace
who does not dodge
life's hard questions

Chapter 1

Abraham Miller came awake with a start. The people in front of him were arguing; their words sharp, intense, hammering in short bursts.

He unfolded himself from the train seat and tried to find a more comfortable position. His long legs had no good place to go except the aisle. He turned sideways, leaned against the cold window, and pulled his flat-brimmed hat lower over his deep brown eyes. The kerosene lamps at each end of the train car were turned low, but their glare still didn't help a man sleep.

Hours of travel had taken him many miles from what was left of his home near Goshen, Indiana. Another twelve hours would pass before he could hope to find a hotel in Council Bluffs on the Missouri River. Train travel sped along very fast, but Abe wasn't so sure it bettered a good horse for convenience and pleasantness. His dad's herd had supplied many proud farmers in Elkhart County for the last twenty years. It made a good living.

At least on a horse, thought Abe as he scratched his short beard, you don't have to be around folks makin' a row. The people in front were still at it, loud enough now that Abe could pick out the words.

"You mean to tell me that Mr. Meacham is no longer the Indian superintendent? How come, Papa?"

"Simmer down, Mary. He wasn't good for us settlers."

"What do you mean, 'wasn't good?' He's been a solid friend of our family for years!"

"*Humpf*," the big man snorted. "Meacham was going to let those Modocs stay on our range."

Abe shifted again in his seat and cleared his throat loudly, hoping that the couple would get the hint. With one finger, he casually tipped up his hat and noticed that other people were also disturbed by the couple's irritating grumble. Across the aisle, the little bald man who had gotten on in Chicago scowled harder until his walrus mustache nearly drooped to the bottom of his chin. Three seats forward two ladies turned around to stare. But the man and woman in front of Abe seemed oblivious to everyone else.

"Well, isn't the Lost River their home?"

"What's come over you, girl? I spend a lot of good money to send you away to school, and you come back with no respect in your talk. Those Indians belong on a reservation. And now Odeneal is gonna put 'em there."

"Who's Odeneal?"

"He's the new superintendent for Oregon—and a good man, too. He'll listen when us settlers tell him the way it has to be."

Abe put his hand on the shoulder of the burly man in front of him. The man's head turned on his bull neck. Squinting eyes looked out from under wiry brows at Abe's hand as though it were a fly, then slowly followed Abe's arm up until they met his eyes.

"Excuse me, sir," Abe said as he quickly withdrew his hand. "But I was wondering if you could . . . well, maybe talk more softly. Some of us are tryin' to get some sleep."

"If you was wantin' sleep, why didn't you take one of them newfangled Pullman cars?" The great head under a too-small, sweat-stained hat turned back around. But the conversation did quiet to a murmur.

Abe pulled his leather case out from under the seat and jammed it into the corner, hoping to make a rest he could lean against. It wasn't much help. Seemed like his body just didn't bend in the right places for most chairs.

Funny how that girl in front reminded him of Amy. His sister had been about the same age—twenty, only a couple years younger than himself. She had the same dark, thick hair around a fair-skinned face, too. He wondered how his sister would have looked if she had ever dressed in anything brighter than their Mennonite black. Now he'd never know.

He had almost drifted off to sleep when the talking got louder again. "So I suppose you just went down to Yreka and wired Washington and told them you wanted Meacham replaced by this . . . this Odeneal fellow?"

"No, as a matter of fact. I had to do a lot more than that. I went all the way back to Washington and saw Kramer. You probably don't remember him from when you were a kid. But it just so happens that he's a squawman. Used to live in Oregon with an Indian wife."

"So?"

"So, now he's got a wife in Washington D.C. . . . from very high society, too. I just reminded Kramer of the wife he left in Oregon, and he was quite ready to recommend to others in the Bureau that Odeneal get the assignment."

"Reno Bauder! That's blackmail! How could you—"

The man's beefy right hand backhanded the girl across the mouth. Several people in the coach screamed. A child started crying. Abe jumped up and grabbed Bauder by the back of his vest and tried to pull him away. Bauder swung around and flung Abe off, pulling back his left for a heavy blow. "You touch me again, kid, and I'll knock your head clean off."

Abe recovered his footing in the swaying train aisle. "You had no right hittin' a lady," he protested, trying to sound confident, but not knowing what he'd actually do if things went any farther.

"This is family and none of your business," growled the man. "I gotta unlearn some of the sass that college put into her."

Abe glanced at the girl. She was dabbing the corner of her lip with a handkerchief. "You okay, ma'am?" he asked, taking a closer look. She's beautiful, he thought, drinking in the dark eyes and lashes in her fair face. No young woman deserved a father like this . . . this animal.

"I-it's all right," she answered. Even in the dim light, Abe could see a blush rise in her cheeks.

"Come on . . . it's over now." The bald man with the walrus mustache stood up beside Abe. "Let's get some air," he said, taking Abe by the arm and drawing him toward the rear of the train. Abe followed, glad for the chance to back out of the situation before it got worse.

Chapter 2

*T*he little man put on a brown bowler, opened the back door, and held it for Abe as they stepped out onto the platform. A blast of cold air hit them. Their coach was last on the train. They stood in silence, watching the silver rails stab out into the December night behind them. The clickity-clack of the wheels and the steady sway of the train put Abe in a daze as the events of the last few minutes stampeded through his mind.

He wanted to smash that Bauder. If he'd just hit him as the man turned around. That would have been the time. His jaw was open for a moment, and Abe was sure he could have put him down . . . But how did he know? He wasn't used to brawling, and that guy was built like an ox. Still, Abe didn't care. At least he could have made a good showing. Bauder might be six foot . . . but Abe was two inches taller, and strong too. He hadn't helped his dad raise horses his whole life for nothing. He should have done it. He should have smashed that beast. Abe's heart was still pounding as he gripped the railing.

". . . I said, my name's Davis, Jonathan Davis. What's yours?"

"Oh, uh . . . excuse me." Abe realized that the little man had been talking to him. "Uh, name's Abraham Miller. Pleased to meet you."

Davis looked him up and down. "Mennonite fellow, aren't ya?" he said with a smile.

Abe knew that he looked typically Mennonite with his black coat and pants sewn from coarse material without any buttons—only the hooks and eyes held the neck of his bloused, gray shirt together—but he had tucked his pants inside his well-made boots and wore his flat hat tipped brashly forward, pulled low over one eye.

He nodded, his deep-set eyes gleaming in the dim light. "I'm from Goshen. Saw you get on at Chicago." Abe's beard softened an otherwise angular face with high cheek bones, straight nose, and a mouth that was hard-lined for someone so young.

He was trying to be friendly to this man who had pulled him out of trouble, but his mind was racing, thinking he should still do something about what happened back inside the train car. The girl's safety was at risk with a man like that Bauder fellow, father or not.

"I didn't think Mennonites were a fightin' people."

"Well, we're not," stammered Abe. "We believe in making peace," he added as an afterthought.

"Peace, huh? Sure looked to me like you were about to lay a *piece* of something on that guy in there. It's good you didn't. He's a western man, used to fightin', I'd say. He'd've ground you up."

Abe didn't answer. Just breathed in the frosty night air. A cloud of heavy smoke blew past. The engine was burning oak. A sliver of a moon hung in the sky and Abe could see a farm off to the south. It was a small place, nothing like home . . . that is, what home had been. Maybe I should have been more friendly to that guy inside, Abe thought. Maybe if I had started talking to those people earlier, I could've changed the subject so they wouldn't have been arguing. I should've done something.

"Where you headin'?" Davis asked.

"Kansas."

"This train won't get you there."

"Yeah, I know," Abe grinned. "I plan to meet a couple men in Council Bluffs. Then we're going down together."

"I'm on my way to Denver," said Davis. "I work for the

Hazard Manufacturing Company. We make Champion Barbwire. Ever hear of us?"

"Can't say as I have."

"Well, we got a big market out west these days. What takes you to Kansas?"

"I'm supposed to be looking over some land for settlin' up a new colony," Abe answered.

"Looking for some space to spread out, are ya? It's good for you young folks to be out there homesteadin' the new lands. I wouldn't mind it myself if I was ten years younger."

"Well, it's not really for me," Abe admitted. "I got as big a place as I'll ever need back home."

"Oh yeah? What do you do?"

"Used to raise horses."

"Who's tending the place for you now?"

"No one. We got wiped out by a tornado last August."

"Gee, that's too bad, kid. Raisin' horses like that, you might consider barbwire for any fence you replace. Your dad busy rebuildin' while you're gone? I'd think he'd need your help."

"He don't need me." Abe didn't want to talk about it.

"Don't get along, huh? I understand; that's why you're off looking elsewhere. Well, that happens. Sometimes it's best . . . " The little man kept talking. Abe didn't want to say any more. But Davis' comment wasn't fair to the memory of his dad.

After a few moments Abe spoke up. "You got it wrong. My dad and I got along fine. It's just that he's gone now. You know . . . the tornado. Him and my whole family."

The little man's jaw dropped. "I . . . I'm sorry kid. I didn't know. Just didn't know or I wouldn't have . . . " Davis stopped as though he didn't know what to say. After a while he said, "Well, I guess I'll get in out of the cold. Comin'?" Abe shook his head. Davis turned and went back into the coach.

Abe stood alone, swaying on the platform. The icy wind ripped through him without a shiver. Always, the violence of the tornado followed him. Yeah, he was on his way to Kansas to get his mind off what had happened and find some peace. But there was none. He couldn't really blame Davis. Davis didn't know. But Abe felt like blaming that Bauder. Yeah, it was Bauder who had broken the peace.

If only things could have been different on that hot day last August.

It had begun as one of those last, lazy dog days, making Abe wonder how many remained before the harvesting and all the work to get ready for winter. The sun was high when he finally hitched up the buckboard and drove off toward Goshen. He would pick up the new hinges from the blacksmith's and the salt from Yoder's, but he was sure he would forget something on the list of items his mother wanted him to get from the store. He kept going over them in his mind: four yards of black broadcloth, the same as she had used for Judith's dress; a bottle of bluing; baking soda; her order of new canning jars . . .

Abe remembered them all when he got to the store. Then he picked up the salt and drove over to the blacksmith's. On the way, he noticed that it had started to cloud up. "Not quite done," Jakob said. "Give me another hour, and you can have the whole set." So Abe stayed around and talked, sometimes pulling on the bellows. Jakob was good. The hinges turned out far better than if Abe or his dad had tried to make them at home.

It was well past noon, and the sky was boiling with dark clouds when Abe started for home. Jakob loaned him a tarp to cover his purchases. The air was heavy and still, only occasionally kicking up little bursts of dust. The sky got darker as Abe hurried the team along. To the south there was a sickly green hue to the clouds. They looked different every time he glanced up.

Drops as big as a robin's egg began to fall—not many, just here and there . . . in the dust of the road, on Abe's nose. His whole knee was wet where just one had hit.

And then he saw it, curling down from the bottom of that

green cloud like a curious, probing finger. Abe slapped the reins harder. He was a mile from home, but his dad would need his help getting the horses in. The funnel hopped along, tickling the earth here and there, and then engaging for a long stretch while it got blacker and swayed like the tail of a stalking cat.

Fear hammered in Abe's chest. The twister was on their farm now, moving right up the creek. He could hear its screaming roar, loud and steady. He whipped the horses into a wild gallop. Their ears were back and their eyes rolled white when they turned their heads. The buckboard hit a chuck hole and nearly flipped over as Abe turned into the lane. Then the twister veered west and came up the rise faster than a runaway herd. When it smashed into the barn, the building exploded like the inside of a thunder clap.

Abe saw boards, hay, and chickens flying everywhere . . . and then the funnel hit the house, but without an explosion. The house existed, and then it did not. The ground was completely clear. Abe could see right through where it had been, across the creek, and to the grove of oaks on the other side where he had hoped to build a house of his own if he ever got married. Why did he think of that right then? The tornado was coming toward him, and he was racing recklessly into its teeth. The wind was picking up, and in a moment it would have him . . . but he didn't care. He had to find his family.

And then it jumped right over him and landed fifty yards behind, ripping up the apple trees along the lane. Abe drove through a roaring, dusty wind. A short stick hit him in the face, cutting his cheek under the right eye. Sticks and dirt and horse manure and straw were falling all around him. He leaped from the buckboard before it had even stopped in the yard and ran toward where the cellar entrance had been. He went only a few steps when an incredible crash behind him shook the earth. He looked back to see his buckboard smashed and the body of their prize mare lying across the wreckage of the right rear wheel. Its abdomen gaped open. Hooves still pawed the air. The team took off in fright, strewing the bloody, dying carcass of the horse behind them.

The mare had fallen from the sky.

Abe turned in shock and walked more cautiously toward where the house had been. Blood was streaming from his cheek. But the cellar was not empty as he had expected. It was full . . . full of the house that had stood so securely for years. It was as though the fist of God had smashed his home right down into a hole in the ground.

Abe remembered digging for hours through the rubble. He finally had to go catch the team and use it to pull the beams off. But he could not remember finding his family, or what had happened that night, or the next day.

His next memory was the graveside with seven coffins lined up. His dad, Matthias J. Miller, had only been forty-five. His mother, Emma, forty-one. Amy had been twenty and beautiful. Ruth, seventeen. Sam, fourteen. Judith, eleven. And little Toby, only three—everybody's favorite.

Everyone died except Abe; he had received no more than a cut on his cheek.

Now he stood on the swaying train platform, rubbing the little scar below his right eye. He held his breath and clinched his eyes . . . trying again to remember finding the bodies. Finally, the air in his lungs burst from his mouth. It was no use. There was nothing he could do. The violence of the storm had taken them. He had seen it coming, but he couldn't do a thing. And now . . . he couldn't even remember.

Davis spoke the truth: Abe was supposed to be a peaceful man . . . like his father . . . like his faith and tradition taught . . . but ever since the tornado, a smoldering rage seethed inside him. Rage against God for what He had done in that one stroke of nature? . . . at himself for failing to get there in time to help? Abe didn't know. But something had changed inside him— something that threatened to burst out of control.

Maybe in Kansas he could forget . . . get away from things that upset him.

The train lurched hard, and Abe realized that they were stopping at a station. He shivered, damp from sweat and very cold. He leaned out from the side of the train and saw buildings and a water tower by the track against the dark sky. Two gas lamps lit the platform, and a sign read, "Grand Junction." After they screeched to a full stop, Abe saw that the engine was taking on water; the train would be here for a few minutes. He stepped down from the little platform and walked toward the station. It looked warm and inviting, and he needed a break.

Chapter 3

*I*nside the Grand Junction station, the lights were cheery, and the pipe on the woodstove in the center glowed red. Abe walked over, welcoming the heat on his hands. The clock ticking on the wall behind the ticket desk showed a quarter past three.

Other passengers from the train came in. Abe noticed Bauder among them. The big man clapped someone on the back and pumped his hand with great joviality. What a sham, Abe thought as he turned back to the stove. If he could just be a little more civil toward that daughter of his . . .

He thought about her again. Were her eyes blue or brown? he wondered. They must be brown, maybe almost black. Yeah, he could remember how they flashed in her fair face, surrounded by that shiny, dark hair. He smiled to himself. She was quite a girl—quite a woman, really, as he recalled her figure.

A hoot sounded from the train whistle, and everyone moved out the door. Abe was one of the last, and the train started to roll as he grabbed the handrail and swung up onto the step of his car.

Inside, he found his seat. Then he noticed Mary Bauder looking anxiously up and down the aisle and out the window to the platform as the end of it slipped past.

"My father . . . did you see my father in there?" she asked him.

"Yeah, I saw him," Abe said. "He was talking to some other guy like they were long-lost friends."

"Yes, but did he get back on the train?"

"Well, I don't know. I suppose he did."

"But he's not here," Mary said. "I must stop the train. They've left him."

Abe looked over at Jonathan Davis and then back to Mary. "Why don't you and Mr. Davis, here, ask the other passengers in our coach if any of them saw your father get back on, and I'll go look for a conductor and see what can be done."

"Oh would you?" she said. "I'd be so grateful. I don't know how we'd meet up again if he missed the train."

"Well, if worse came to worst, you could always meet him again in Omaha," Davis suggested. "You could lay over there and catch him when he arrived on the next train."

Davis got out of his seat and came over to Mary as Abe walked up the aisle and went through the door. He crossed the gap between the platforms and entered the next car. It was a Pullman sleeper. The curtains were all down, and there was no conductor. He walked on through the car, tripping over someone's boots that stuck out into the dark, narrow aisle.

The next car was a coach like his own. However, more people were awake and talking. Near the front of the car, he saw the conductor, his head nodding as he sat alone in his seat.

"Excuse me, sir," Abe said when he got to him. "But I think we'll have to stop the train. We left someone back at the last stop."

"You what?" the conductor said as he jerked awake.

"We left someone at the last stop."

"Who was it?"

"A man . . . a big man. I think his name is Bauder." Abe gestured with his hands the width and height of Bauder.

"Sorry," the conductor said. "Can't stop the train 'cept in an emergency. Besides, if he's as big a man as you say, he can probably take care of himself." The conductor adjusted himself back into his seat and closed his eyes.

"But, sir," Abe said, "you don't understand. He's got a daughter, and now they're separated. She's very upset."

The conductor came alert again. "He has a child on the train?"

"Not a little girl. His daughter. She's a grown woman."

"Forget it, kid. I'm not stopping the train. If he didn't get on, it's his own fault. The whistle blew. Everybody else got on. Now just go on back to your seat." He slumped down in his seat.

"What am I supposed to tell his daughter?" Abe persisted.

"Tell her whatever you want, but I'm not stopping the train. We're at least two miles down the track by now. You want us to back up all that way?" The man hesitated a moment, looking up at Abe who still wasn't leaving. "All right," he sighed, "tell ya what I'll do." He stood up. "Let's go talk to this woman and see what she wants to do. Then I'll send a wire from New Jefferson or Scranton. Is that good enough for you?"

"Thank you, sir," Abe said as they started down the aisle with the conductor walking ahead.

But before they left the conductor's car, Abe saw Reno Bauder. He sat in the last row of seats, under the dim light cast by the rear lamp. Apparently, Abe had missed him earlier because he'd been looking for the conductor. But there he sat, big as life, smoking a cigar and talking to the man Abe had seen him with in the Grand Junction station.

The conductor had almost reached the rear door when Abe reached out and caught his arm. "That's okay, conductor. The man I'm looking for is right here," he said, pointing at Bauder.

Bauder looked up at Abe and squinted his eyes slightly. "Well, I'll be hornswoggled," he snorted. "I thought you'd seen enough of me." He turned away, talking again to his friend.

"Sir . . . " the conductor said.

But Bauder ignored him, gesturing expansively with his hands. "I tell ya, Joe, we had to skid those logs a good two miles before we got them to the river. I nearly did in my horses. Should've had oxen."

"Excuse me, sir," the conductor tried again. "This man was

worried about you."

Bauder slowly turned his head and looked up at Abe and the conductor with bland boredom. "Listen, kid, I can take care of myself. Should think you'd know that by now. Now why don't you go back to your seat and go to sleep."

"Not worried about you, Bauder. It's your daughter."

"Mary?" Bauder's face flipped to cold steel. He came up out of his seat, moving the conductor aside with his arm. He looked straight into Abe's eyes. "What about her? What's happened?" He grabbed Abe's arm with an iron grip.

"Take it easy . . . she's okay. You got no call to get upset," Abe said. "She thought you got left back at Grand Junction. She wanted me to get the conductor to stop the train."

"Stop the train?"

"Yeah, so we could go back and pick you up."

"I told him, sir, that there was no way we could do that," put in the conductor.

Bauder swore sourly as his face reddened with embarrassment. "Who do you think you are, kid—a public chaperone or something? Don't you think people can handle their own affairs? Here you are meddling again."

"Yeah, but . . ."

"Yeah but nothin'," Bauder cut Abe off. "You listen to me. You stay out of my way. I don't want to hear or see anything of you the rest of this trip. Do you understand?"

"But I was just trying—"

"I said, I don't want to hear anymore. Now get out of here." Bauder gestured with his thumb toward the back of the car.

Abe shrugged, squeezed past the conductor, and jerked open the door.

A moment later he stood on the platform between the cars, shaking his head. He had never in his life run into anyone as cantankerous as Bauder. It was absolutely hopeless to try and relate to the man. Abe wondered how anyone else could get along with him. How could he possibly be a successful rancher? And what kind of woman would have married a man like that?

When Abe got back to his car, he simply told Mary that her father was safely on the train, talking to the man he'd seen him with at the station. She thanked him with great relief and settled back into her seat.

But Abe had to tell someone about what happened. He lowered himself into the seat beside Davis and recounted the story in a low voice. Jonathan listened to the report without commenting. Then he said, "I know the kind of man Bauder is. Actually, I think we'd be surprised if we knew how many people are like that underneath. It's civilization . . . civilization is the only thing that restrains his kind. The law holds some back. Public opinion holds others back. But out on the frontier there is no law and order, not really anyway. A man gets used to livin' as he pleases, like water seeking its own level."

"But I've never known anybody like that," Abe said. "Oh, when I used to go into town as a kid, sometimes a bunch of guys used to poke fun at us Mennonites. I'd get plenty mad, but if you ever met any of 'em by themselves, they were usually okay."

"But don't ya see? That's just it," Davis said. "When they were in a group, they had the power to behave as they pleased. But when you met them alone, they weren't quite so brave. That's all I'm sayin'—when restraints are absent, you'll find there are many people who are little better than savages."

Abe shook his head. "I don't know. I've just never met anyone like that Bauder."

"Of course you haven't. First of all, you're a Mennonite . . . spent most of your life among peace-loving people. Second, you live in the most civilized half of the country. As for the other half . . . that's why people pack guns out west. You wait. Even in Kansas you'll see what I mean. Now Bauder . . . Bauder's from Oregon. There are parts out there that are pure wilderness, never been seen by a white man. Bauder's probably used to runnin' the whole show."

"You ever been to Oregon?"

"Nope. Not yet. But that's one place I'd sure like to go."

"How come? You don't sound like you appreciate this law-lessness you're talking about."

"Oh, I don't . . . I don't. But it's the country itself, what I've heard of it, that makes me want to go. Virgin forests . . . wide open valleys . . . breathtaking mountains. And don't get me wrong. There're plenty of good people out west, too. And where there are good people, they'll bring the law sooner or later, and then Bauder's kind will settle down or move on."

"I don't know," said Abe. "Seems like a body could appeal to the good in a man like Bauder and convince him to change his ways."

"Good in a man like Bauder?" Davis laughed. "Miller, you sound like a fool preacher. If there's any good in his kind, it's buried where no one can find it. Believe me, civilization is the only fence for an old bull like him."

Abe's eyelids felt like they had lead weights on them. "Maybe so," he said, stifling a yawn. "Well, see you in the morning." He got up and moved over to his own seat. This time, in spite of the cramped space, he fell asleep quickly.

• • •

When he awoke, the winter sun had come up and the conductor was announcing the next stop. "Dunlap! Next station is Dunlap!" Good. There'd be fifteen minutes for breakfast.

The biscuits and gravy were cold, but the coffee was strong and hot. Abe ate standing at a counter between several other men. Women and families shared the few tables. There was hardly time to finish before the whistle called everyone back to the train.

Bauder still hadn't returned to his seat beside Mary as the train got underway. Abe wanted to talk to her . . . get to know her. So far all he knew was what he'd overheard. Abe took off his hat and leaned forward toward the back of Mary's seat. He started to speak but then stopped, looked down, and spun his hat in his hands.

Chapter 4

*F*inally Abe stopped spinning his hat in his hands and cleared his throat. "Excuse me, Miss. We haven't been introduced, but . . ."

Mary turned around. "No we haven't. My name is Mary Bauder, and Mr. Davis said your name was Abraham Miller." She stated it as a fact, and Abe couldn't figure whether she was inviting more conversation or not. But she didn't turn back.

"Well, I . . . Miss Bauder, I was wondering if we could talk, get to know each other a little better, seeing as how we . . . well, since so much happened during the night."

"I suppose so. I'm sorry about my father. He's just . . . " She said no more but kept looking at him with her dark, unblinking eyes. Abe looked down at his hat that was spinning faster and faster. He almost dropped it before he ventured to look up at her again.

"I'm from Indiana . . . Goshen, Indiana, that is, and I'm on my way to Kansas."

"I'm on my way home to Oregon. I've been at school for two and a half years—at Barat College, north of Chicago a ways."

"College?" Abe said . . . then remembered Bauder had accused her of learning "sass" at college.

"Yes . . . a women's college. I had hoped to finish, but my father requires my help at home." She paused. "Mr. Miller, I don't mind talking to you, but I'd rather not stay twisted in my seat like this."

"Oh. Of course not. Please excuse me," Abe said, slipping his hat on and leaning back in his seat.

"That's not what I mean," she said patiently. "Why don't you move up here beside me, and then you can tell me why you're going to Kansas."

Abe made the move, excited that she was willing to talk more. He took his hat off again. "Well," he said self-consciously, "as you probably can guess, I'm from a Mennonite community, and Daniel Brenneman—he's one of the elders in the Mennonite Church—asked me to make a trip with a couple other men to look for a new colony. There's been a lot of our folks who want to start some new colonies farther west. Some say Kansas would be a good place, what with the railroad opening the territory and all . . . Also, there're thousands of Russian Mennonites fixin' to come over to this country soon, and they'll be needin' land they can farm. If we can find good locations for colonies, it will help them—"

Mary's laugh cut into his stream of words. "What do you mean, starting a colony? Has some king commissioned you?" she teased, sitting up very straight and proper. "I thought Kansas was part of the United States."

Abe chuckled. He liked being teased by this girl. "I'm not talking about a colony like the Thirteen Colonies. It's just that our people always like to live near each other, so that we can help each other out and be near a meetinghouse. Mennonites have been in Indiana a long time, and there's not much more room for new farms—at least not nearby."

"Are you looking for a new farm, too?"

"No . . . no. I've got a big enough one back home."

"You live with your folks?"

Abe turned and looked out the window across the aisle. "I used to," he said as he turned back to look at his hat in his lap. "My family got killed in a tornado last summer." Abe hadn't meant to tell Mary about his family, but somehow it had come out before he had time to think.

"I'm sorry," said Mary softly. "My mother died almost three years ago. I know how you must feel."

"But it was my *whole* family," Abe said quickly.

Mary nodded. "That must have been terrible. I-I never had any brothers or sisters myself."

They sat silently for a few moments. Abe realized that Mary had essentially lost her whole family too. Certainly with a father like her's, she wasn't left with much to cherish in the way of family. He looked at her and nodded slightly. He could believe that she did understand; he didn't need to say more. There was more peace in her eyes than he had experienced for months.

"Is that when you came back here to school . . . because of your mother's death, I mean?" Abe asked.

"Yes. At the time, my father . . . well, it had always been my mother's wish for me to go to school. She was an educated woman herself, and . . . I didn't want to stay at home with her gone."

"But you're going back now."

"Yes."

"Why?"

"I told you. My father came and got me. He says he needs me."

"Do you want to go back?"

"I don't know. Not really, I guess. I wanted to finish school."

"Are you afraid?"

"Why do you ask that?" Mary challenged quickly.

"Well, I don't think I was dreaming last night."

"Oh. Well, maybe a little. My father seems to have changed. Though, he always was rough. But . . . I'll be okay."

"Has he ever hit you before?"

"No . . . not like that. But when I was a little girl, he was gone a lot of the time. My grandpa lived with us then, and he was very kind. I can't really remember very well, but my folks had some terrible arguments. I think my father sometimes hit Momma. I know when he was angry, she would kinda keep me away from him. I never got to know him very well. Never really wanted to, I guess."

They rode in silence for a couple minutes. Finally Mary said, "Tell me what you'll look for in Kansas. Why did this Mr. Brenneman send you?"

Abe didn't answer. He was thinking about Bauder slapping Mary in the night. It was so sudden, so unfair. What would he do when he was off in those hills of Oregon alone with this woman? If Davis was right—that civilization restrained a man's savagery—what would restrain him when he was out of sight of the people on the train? Abe imagined Bauder as a wild mountain man, dressed in smelly, grease-stained buckskins, living in a makeshift lean-to or even a cave. Mary would be forced to slave for him . . . maybe even worse. Abe caught his spinning thoughts . . . No, even Bauder'd never do that. But then, he had hit her right in public, and she a grown woman. His heart was pounding with rage . . .

"Abe, Abe." Mary's hand was resting gently on his arm. "What are you thinking about, anyway?" She laughed lightly. "You seem a thousand miles away."

Her beauty was like the surface of a small lake, surprisingly different in every mood—deep with changing color, shimmering in the bright sun, clear, placid, reflective. He could gaze at her forever. But he turned away. "I'm sorry. I was just thinking about you having to live in the wilds of Oregon, so far from civilization."

"It's not so bad. The ranch is really one of the most beautiful places you can imagine, and our house is very comfortable. Momma and I used to get into town twice a month or so. Except when the roads were bad, you could make it in a two-hour ride."

"Town? Is there a town out there?"

"Of course there is." Her eyes twinkled as she smiled at Abe's notions about the West. "Linkville has several families and a hotel." She paused, gaging Abe's response. "We even have a restaurant, a livery, and a schoolhouse. A Methodist minister comes by once a month to hold services. There's probably more that's been built up since I was there. And Fort Klamath is only about fifty miles north of us."

"Well, I'm glad to hear it." Abe tried to modify his fantasies about her living in a cave, waiting on a foul mountain man. He could change the setting in his mind's eye, but not the situation of danger for Mary.

"What about Indians? Your father said there was Indian trouble."

Mary shrugged. "There's always been problems. Our ranch is right on Lost River, and that's been their home for generations. But Superintendent Meacham was always able to settle things. If the Modocs had a complaint, he'd have us give them a beef every now and then. And if they stole something from us—which they did sometimes—well, Meacham just made them pay with a horse or a few days work around our place. They're actually good people—most of them anyway."

"But it sounds like things have changed now."

"Maybe, but it'll work out. The old days are gone. The Modocs all wear the white man's clothes now, and most of them speak English. Of course, it didn't use to be that way. They were one of the fiercest tribes in the West." Mary stopped and turned to gaze out the window.

Anxious to know her thoughts, Abe said, "And . . . ?"

When Mary continued, her voice sounded distant, like she was dreaming. "There are stories of them attacking some of the early wagon trains, including the one that brought my father out west . . . One place is still called Bloody Point, near Tule Lake. The teamsters were just circling the wagons for the night. No one had a notion of trouble . . . Then off the rimrock came a whole party of screaming warriors. Dad says the emigrants fought bravely . . . but I guess they didn't have a chance. Dad was wounded and apparently fell unconscious into some tall tules along the lake shore . . ."

Mary turned back to Abe. "He was the only survivor out of

eighty people. Wagons were burned . . . men, women, and children mutilated . . . Dad staggered out and made it all the way to Jacksonville for help. When rescuers returned to the site . . ." Mary shuddered. " . . . there was a pile of babies with their heads smashed against a large rock."

Abe was stunned. He'd never heard of such a horrible thing. "What . . . what did your dad do?"

"Oh, he went right on with life as soon as his wounds healed. But I don't know that he's ever really recovered."

"What do you mean?"

"Well, it wasn't long after that that he married my mother. And then, when I was born in 1852, we homesteaded right there on Lost River. I would have thought he had all the hate out of his system by then . . . but it seems to grow bigger by the year."

"What do you mean about him getting it all out of his system?"

"Of course, I don't remember any of this, but a few months before we homesteaded, Dad went down to Lost River with a group of men that Ben Wright had organized from Rogue River, Oregon." As Mary spoke, a bitter frown tightened her face. "They invited the Modocs to a peace council near Natural Bridge—real close to where our ranch is now. About forty-five men and a few squaws came." Mary looked down at her hands. Finally she quietly said, "Only five Indians were alive the next morning to escape. They even killed the women and children."

Abe stared at her. "But that's as savage as what the Indians did!"

"My father called it justice."

"Your father didn't take part in it, did he?"

"Well, Momma and I never knew anything about it or how we got the land our house is on until years later. My father never did say whether he did any of the killing or not. All he'd say was, 'We had to strike while the iron was hot. It whittled down their numbers and kept them peaceful all these years.' The only other thing I remember about it was that my folks often argued about it . . . that is, how he got the land and all."

"Why didn't something like that lead to war?"

"Oh, there have been incidents, but that massacre killed a lot of Indians, including their chief. I guess they were just 'subdued,' as Dad calls it. They were without a chief for years," Mary said.

"Do they have one now?"

"Yes, finally. He's the son of the old chief who died in the massacre. His name is Kintpuash. I've met him a couple times. Most whites call him Captain Jack because he likes to wear cast-off army uniforms."

"Is he peaceful?" asked Abe.

"I think so. He signed a peace treaty to move his people onto a reservation several years ago, but there's been some dispute about the government changing the terms of the treaty or something. Anyway, the Modocs are still at Lost River. But like I said, it's their home."

The conversation drifted to other subjects . . . what she had been studying in school . . . Abe's plan to meet Jonas Showalter and Noah Eby in Council Bluffs and go to Kansas. Abe told Mary about his interest in writing. He got his leather travel bag and dug out the two copies of the *Herald of Truth* he kept carefully in the bottom under his Bible. "Here," he said as he unfolded the already brittle sheets of the church newspaper. "I wrote this report about buildin' the Yoder's barn. And in this issue, John F. Funk—he's the editor—well, he printed my essay on 'The Way of Peace.' He says he thinks I could become a good writer. I'm supposed to send back reports about what we find in Kansas. If it's good, he'll print it."

After what seemed like mere minutes they heard the conductor call out, "Council Bluffs comin' up! End of the line for the Chicago and Northwestern Railway. Everyone off. Connections for points west via the transfer train. Points south, the Council Bluffs Railroad . . ."

Abe didn't listen anymore. The time had come when he had to leave Mary, but . . . he didn't want to. He was worried about her safety. He wanted to become better acquainted with her, look into those deep dark eyes that drew him on, feel the touch of her hand on his arm again. He wanted to hear more of her laugh that made his own heart so light. It was no time to say good-bye.

"Abe, would you help me get my luggage? My cape is up there, and I have two bags. I don't know where my father is."

He loved to hear her call him "Abe." He wished he had the courage to call her "Mary." Instead, he said, "I'd be glad to, Miss Bauder."

The confusion when they got off the train was near pandemonium. Everyone had to remove all their own luggage from the train and get aboard the transfer train that would take them across the Missouri River. Then they would again unload and reload onto the Union Pacific heading west.

Jonathan Davis had gotten off the train with Abe and Mary. "Politics. That's all this transfer train business is," he muttered. "Union Pacific doesn't want to pay the expense of maintaining the bridge. But someday, I bet they'll keep the same cars from New York to San Francisco. They might change engines, but the passengers won't have to suffer all this trouble."

Just then they heard Bauder bellowing Mary's name from somewhere down the platform. They hurried in his direction till they caught sight of him. Bauder took Mary's bags from Abe without a word of greeting or thanks, then turned and headed off toward the transfer train alone.

"I've got to go," Mary said, offering her hand to Abe. "Thank you ever so much for all the help you've been."

"You're quite welcome," Abe fumbled. "I hope you have a pleasant trip."

"And I hope you find what you're looking for in Kansas."

She had left her hand in his a little longer than necessary—

at least, it seemed that way to Abe. "Good-bye, Mary," he called as she hurried off.

Davis hung behind as Abe watched Mary's stately form move on after her father. "He's a real cuss, isn't he?" Davis said. "He walks off like she's a puppy dog that's supposed to follow him."

"He's an animal!" Abe said vehemently. "He has no right makin' her go with him. Listen, Davis. You're going to be on that train for a couple more days. Do me a favor . . . look out for her, would ya?"

"Well, sure, Miller. I'll keep an eye on her, but I don't know what good it'll do."

"I'm serious Davis. I'm really worried. She doesn't want to be with him, and she shouldn't have to."

"Well, now, you know there's nothin' I can do about that. It usually doesn't pay to go interfering in family matters . . . Hey, I gotta go. Take care, okay, kid? And if you ever need any barb-wire, look me up." Davis hurried away and hopped aboard the transfer train just as it began to pull out.

Abe hesitated, glancing once more down the train to the coach Mary and her father had boarded. He felt uneasy . . . But there are some things a man can't change, he told himself, and I'm bound for Kansas. But as he picked up his bag and started to leave the train station, he wasn't so sure there was nothing he could do.

Chapter 5

*T*hat night Abe got very little sleep in his hotel room in Council Bluffs. He blamed the damp, moldy smell of his bed and the coal smoke that boiled from the end of the short stovepipe just outside his window.

When he was awake, he daydreamed of showing Mary his farm—riding across the open fields or having a picnic by a stream. But when he was asleep, his dreams ricocheted between Bauder's yelling and Mary fleeing wild Indians.

"This is crazy," Abe said to himself as he sat up in bed. "Why do I keep thinking about her?" He lay back down again and stayed very still in the dark for a few minutes.

Suddenly, he threw off the blanket and swung his legs onto the floor. The warped, rough boards were cold and gritty under his feet. He groped for the candle on the chair beside his bed and lit it. He dug the family Bible out of the leather bag and thumbed through it, looking at various underlined passages until he stopped at one: "Be careful for nothing; but in every thing by prayer and supplication with thanksgiving let your requests be made known unto God. And the peace of God, which passeth all understanding, shall keep your hearts and minds through Christ Jesus."

He closed the book with a thud. "Hollow comfort that is," he muttered. "God, thanks for keeping me safe traveling on a train. Requests: Let's see. Help me to forget about this nonsense and get some sleep. Amen." He blew out the candle and flopped down.

"Be anxious for nothing," he told himself, but it didn't work.

He drifted in and out of a fitful sleep for the next few hours and finally gave up at dawn.

After washing up and having breakfast, Abe felt better and went out for a walk. In the daylight, he knew he had been rather flippant with God, using a verse to demand easy sleep. Maybe he should tell God he was sorry, he thought. But as he wandered down the street, looking at store windows, nodding and smiling at the townspeople going about their morning business, he never got around to praying.

The men he was supposed to meet—Showalter and Eby—should be arriving soon, he thought, and the day was clear and pleasant. At nighttime, the early winter cold froze the gnarled mud street into a cobbled path. During the day, wagon wheels and hooves and boots worked it incessantly, turning it into a mire wherever the sun hit it.

He bought a newspaper and headed back toward the river just in time to see a boat dock. Two men came walking up the bank in flat-brimmed hats and matching, black clothes. There was no doubt about who they were. Abe introduced himself and shook hands.

Jonas Showalter was nearly as tall as Abe, a heavy, warm man. Abe guessed him to be close to fifty, though his gray, thin hair made him look older. Noah Eby was shorter and more slight. He had a pinched face, hollow eyes, and a wispy beard growing mostly from the end of his chin. He looked younger than Showalter by maybe ten years, but when he laughed and grinned, which he did often, there wasn't a tooth in his mouth. Eby was the spokesman, and Abe soon found out why. Showalter preferred to speak German—with a dialect that Abe had trouble understanding. Finally Abe had to ask him to use English or have Eby translate.

Noon found the trio enjoying bowls of chili in the little cafe across from Abe's hotel. Except for occasional comments Showalter tried to insert, Eby talked almost nonstop until they boarded the train heading toward Kansas. He filled Abe in on every detail of their trip and all that they had explored in Minnesota.

The train wasn't crowded, and they found seats facing each other. Jonas and Noah sat together; Abe sat across from them, next to the window. He piled some of their things on the seat beside him.

When they were finally rolling south toward St. Joseph, Eby said, "Well, Abe, what do you think? We think Mountain Lake is the place to recommend for a new colony. It's got the best soil a farmer could ask for." He stopped, waiting for Abe's response.

"I don't know, Noah. Minnesota sounds like a good place to me . . . from what you say. But I wasn't there, so what can I say? And besides, if it's so good, why are we going down to Kansas?"

"Oh, we to Kansas are still going," said Jonas in his broken English. "It was the plan to survey both. So, we do it."

"Well, I don't suppose we'd have to," countered Noah. "The plan was to find a good place for a colony, and we found one. As for me, I'm puttin' in for Minnesota. I got just the place picked. Still, Matthew Keim is expecting us to meet him in Newton. He's a Pennsylvania Mennonite, I hear. Did you know he's bought up five thousand acres of land from Case and Billings? Hopes to sell off pieces to the rest of us when we start a colony. I saw one of his letters. Said he bought it so we could be sure of getting places near each other. He's offering it for $2.50 an acre. But I don't know. I think I'd rather choose for myself."

Jonas cleared his throat. "I think we rest in quietness awhile on the idea. Leave God to lead us. We are going now anyway."

"I guess you're right," Noah said with one of his toothless grins.

The men sat back and watched the majestic Missouri as the train snaked them along its eastern bank. In places the water churned white with foam, then opened out with hardly a ripple in its brown surface. In the backwaters there were still hundreds of geese and ducks, pausing on their way south. It was an open, mostly unsettled country, and the stops along the way were short. The train took on a passenger or two here and there and of course wood and water. At Hamburg there was time for a cup of strong, black coffee and some apple pie.

In the late afternoon, Abe drew out the newspaper he had purchased back at Council Bluffs. It was *The New York Times*, dated December 1, 1872—only two days old. He scanned several articles, reading reports from correspondents in France on the turbulent crisis there, commentaries on problems in Washington, and a description of a new expedition planned for the Amazon.

Then the title of a news report leaped out at him.

MODOC UPRISING
Savages Massacre
a Dozen Settlers on Lost River

YREKA, CAL. Nov. 31—A courier has arrived here from Lost River on the Oregon/California boarder with the sad news that the long-feared Indian war with the savage Modoc Indians has begun with the ambush and slaying of 12 settlers in the last 48 hours.

In the night of November 28, Captain Jackson and 40 soldiers from Fort Klamath plus ten civilian volunteers quietly made their way into the Modoc camp along Lost River. The purpose was to persuade the Indians to surrender and return to the Klamath Reservation.

Here, in the Captain's own words is the story:

"I have the honor to report that I jumped the camp of Captain Jack's Modoc Indians soon after dawn, completely surprising them. I demanded their surrender and disarming, and asked for a parley with Captain Jack. Captain Jack, Scarfaced Charley, Black Jim, and some others, would neither lay down their arms nor surrender, and some of them commenced making hostile demonstrations against us. We were forced to respond. From somewhere a shot rang out, and being a wise strategist, I took no chances but immediately opened fire. We poured volley after volley among the hostiles, took their camp, killed eight or nine, and drove the rest into the hills.

"One citizen was killed during the fight (Mr. Nuss) and another (Joe Pennig) badly wounded. One soldier was killed and several wounded.

"My force was too weak to pursue and capture the Indians that made off, owing to the necessity of taking immediate care of my wounded. We took over the near-by Bauder ranch . . ."

Abe looked at the name in shock: "the near-by Bauder ranch." That had to be Mary's home! There was no other possibility: it was Oregon . . . the Lost River . . . Modoc Indians. He read on.

". . . We took over the near-by Bauder ranch to make a temporary infirmary.

"It was from this location that I learned that some of the hostiles had regrouped and were attacking neighboring ranches."

So far, at least a dozen settlers have been killed by the renegades.

The Indian war that so many have predicted has commenced. Many persons believe the Modocs are utterly desperate and will fight till their last man falls before leaving the Lava Beds where they have taken refuge.

However the new superintendent, "No-nonsense" Odeneal, disagrees: "I'm confident that the Indians can be dislodged easily, as soon as a small force can be dispatched to pursue them. We'll clean them out and send them to the reservation."

T. B. Odeneal has recently replaced the former Indian superintendent for the region, A. B. Meacham.

Abe sat staring at the paper, his eyes racing back over the words. "It can't be," he mumbled under his breath. "Mary's returning home right into the middle of an Indian war."

"Abe? What's the matter?" said Noah.

Abe quickly closed the paper and tucked it down beside him. "It ain't nothin'."

"You look like you're gettin' sick. I got a cousin who gets sick anytime he rides a wagon or a buggy or anything but a horse. I bet he'd be sick on this train, too."

"It ain't the train . . . I'm okay."

"Yeah, but you look white as talcum," pressed Noah.

"I'm all right. Just forget it, okay?"

Noah shrugged and turned. Soon, he was amused by the antics of a small boy in the seat across the aisle.

But Abe couldn't follow his own advice. He couldn't forget it. He couldn't just let Mary Bauder walk unsuspecting into an Indian war! His mind was racing, nagged by something that had happened earlier on the train . . . something Bauder said just before he hit Mary. But Abe couldn't remember. He reviewed the events in his mind. They had wakened him with their arguing about the Indians. Mary had been upset about something her father had done . . . Now it was coming to him. It had to do with those two superintendents, the same ones mentioned in the paper.

Blackmail. That was it. Mary had said Bauder used blackmail to get Meacham fired and replaced by Odeneal.

Abe remembered Bauder saying, "Meacham was going to let those Modocs stay on our range." But this Odeneal—the paper called him "No-nonsense" Odeneal . . . Bauder had been counting on him to get the Indians off the ranch!

The implications were caving in on Abe. Bauder's actions smacked of far more than a little bureaucratic corruption. It was beginning to sound like a conspiracy for starting a war—a war in which people were already dying, a war into which he was dragging his daughter.

Abe realized he was breathing hard, his jaw and fists clenched tight. Pretty soon Noah would ask him again what the matter was.

He looked out the window trying to concentrate on the scenery. But it was no use. His mind kept spinning while his eyes stared at the river which looked now like a wide sheet of polished copper. The sun had set, leaving the sky and water the color of a roaring fire . . . fire and charred wood. The bare, black branches that fled past the window, the little dock out in the water, and the narrow strip of ragged land on the other side—they seemed lifeless, dark, devoid of color. Only the sky and water were alive. They were so brilliant that they hurt Abe's eyes.

A rowboat was making its way up the river to the dock. The charcoal-colored fisherman rowed slowly, leaving a trail of darkness spreading out on the glassy river behind him.

Abe sat looking out the window mile after mile without really seeing anything. A great blue heron got his attention as it rose up from the water and kept perfect pace with the train. It flew even with Abe's window and not so far out on the water. The beauty of it induced a mystic melancholy at the center of his soul. He marveled at how slow and easy the bird worked its huge wings to slice through the now-crimson sky.

Then the train turned away from the bird and river . . . and thoughts about Bauder and the "Modoc uprising" crashed once more into his consciousness. Abe wished he could stay by the river . . . the scene was so peaceful, that it was easy to pretend everything was all right. But the train hurried on. Unfortunately, it was carrying him farther and farther away from Mary . . . who was riding another train straight into danger.

Chapter 6

*T*he train pulled into St. Joseph late that night. Abe and the two older men spent the night—what was left of it—at a hotel and caught the Atchison, Topeka & Santa Fe the next morning. The sun had already set the next evening before they arrived in Newton, Kansas.

All that way, Abe fought to keep himself from dwelling on Bauder. He was sure Showalter and Eby wouldn't understand. If he told them how he was feeling, he'd have to tell them about the incident on the train and how close he had come to hitting Bauder. Even now he wanted the man dead. Davis had been right. There was no room for Bauder's kind of violence among civilized people. The thoughts ground together in Abe's mind, but he didn't dare let his two Mennonite companions know . . . certainly not when he was out here on a mission for the church.

Newton had been a roaring cow town, with slapped-up, bare-board, false-fronted buildings that lined a wide main street. The train station was the only structure in town with plastered walls. The townspeople lived in a variety of shacks, shanties, and tents, set up wherever they pleased with no concern for laying out proper streets—except the main street.

The town had boomed from almost nothing just two years before to shipping hundreds of thousands of cattle east. The pens could hold six thousand longhorns, and six railcars could be loaded at a time. But life quieted down just as quickly when the train pushed a spur twenty-eight miles south to Wichita, giving the Texas cattle drivers a closer railhead to load their beef.

The people who had stayed in Newton were a more settled type. Some cattle were still shipped from there, but many new farmers had also arrived. The race to complete the railroad west to Colorado was in full swing, and all the men, equipment, and supplies passed through Newton. If the Santa Fe completed the job by its March deadline, it would win the government land grant. Rumor had it that the crew would beat the deadline and complete the line before the end of the year. Newton would last; it even had a marshal—something it lacked the year before when more than two dozen people were shot. Still, the marshal was a busy man.

Matthew Keim was not at the station when Abe, Noah, and Jonas arrived. Noah suggested they get something to eat while they waited, but halfway through his steak, Abe stood up.

"I wonder if you brothers would excuse me, I need to get some air."

"I told you, you weren't feeling well," said Noah, jabbing a finger at him. "It's that train what did it."

"Maybe," Abe nodded vaguely. Once outside, he started to walk down the main street, but the noise blaring from the several saloons deterred him. Instead, he cut behind a building called Horner's Store. The twilight was still bright enough that he could find his way between the piles of firewood, a corral, wagon, and various farm implements. Other than a few shacks with dim lights in their windows, he was completely alone . . . and could think.

"Already twelve settlers dead," muttered Abe as he kicked at a stone in his path. "And that was nearly a week ago." He wondered if there was any way of getting a more recent paper in Newton. How could he reach Mary and warn her? She was days ahead of him on the train. He could try the telegraph but to what station would he send it? Even if he could figure out where Mary and her father would get off the train, chances were high that Bauder would intercept the message.

Bauder was the culprit. If it weren't for him, the war

wouldn't have started and Mary wouldn't be heading into danger. I should have gotten Mary away from him . . . I should have stopped him . . . I should have smashed him right then—it might have given her the courage to resist, Abe thought, breathing hard, grinding his right fist into his left palm.

Just then a dark figure stepped out from between two buildings about twenty yards in front of him. The man was walking slowly and swaying a little. Abe held back, not wanting to surrender his solitude. And then, another figure came up behind the first. There was a brief scuffle, and the first man went down. Abe started forward. The man on the ground was moaning; the one above going through his pockets. A dog from a nearby shanty started barking.

"Hey, whatcha doin'?" Abe challenged.

The second man jumped back and pulled a gun. In his other hand glinted a bright watch and a fat money bag. "Just take it easy, kid, and nobody gets hurt." He pointed his six-shooter right at Abe as he took another step back.

Abe moved forward and knelt over the man on the ground. Weak moans were coming from him. And there, right on the man's hip was a holstered gun. "It's gotta stop," muttered Abe. On impulse he grabbed the gun, brought it up . . . then he heard a tremendous explosion.

For a moment Abe couldn't see. He stood up and realized that the robber wasn't there. He wasn't standing . . . he wasn't lying on the ground. He was just gone. The robbery victim was coming to, still moaning, but holding his head and trying to sit up.

The back door of the next building flung open, and a shaft of light shone out. Framed in the doorway stood a man with a white towel wrapped around his waist and tucked into his pants. "What's going on out here? . . . Hey, Jeb," he called back into the noisy saloon, "better come take a look."

"You okay?" asked Abe as he leaned down to help the man up. And then he noticed his own hand. In the dark, there wasn't much color, but great dark streaks were flowing down and dripping off his fingertips. He'd been shot. He'd been shot right in the hand. It wasn't hurting yet, but there it was. No question. Blood running all over the place.

As the man on the ground stood up, holding his head and brushing off his clothes, two men came out of the saloon. Abe figured that the one with the towel was the barkeep. The other's face was hidden under a wide-brimmed hat.

"Awright, I sport the badge around here," said the man with the hat. "What happened? . . . Oh, it's you, Mr. Carter. You all right?" The marshal took a couple swipes at dusting the victim's suit. Abe could see that it was well tailored.

"I think I'm all right . . . 'cept I got a pretty big egg on my head, and a brass band's still playing in my ears."

"Who's this other fella?" the marshal said, indicating Abe.

"I don't know," said Carter. "He was here when I came to."

"He was leaning over Mr. Carter when I looked out," volunteered the bartender.

"The name's Abraham Miller. Uh, I just got into town on the train and I was—"

"What business you got prowling around out here at night? . . . Say, what's this? You shoot this guy, Mr. Carter? He's got blood dripping all over."

"Not me, Jeb. Like I said, I was out cold."

"It was the robber—" started Abe.

"Robbed?" said Carter, feeling his pockets. "Hey! I was robbed. He got my money, and . . . my gold watch, and . . . and my gun."

"No, I have your gun . . ." Abe stopped. "Or at least, I had it." The gun wasn't in his hand anymore, but he had actually drawn a gun on someone, intending to use it. The reality hit him like a train. "I . . . I guess it got shot out of my hand."

"Here it is, over here," said the bartender, picking it out of the dust several feet away. He stuffed the big pistol in his belt.

"All right," said the marshal. "Let's get inside where we can figure this out. But for the moment, consider yourself under arrest, Mr. whatever-your-name-is."

Inside the saloon, the bartender whipped off his towel and threw it on the counter. "All right, bar's closed!" he called out.

"Gilmer, you're worse than a fickle range cow. No one can tell whether you're wet or dry," said one of the hands at the bar. "Let us set up for ourselves."

"Not a chance," growled Gilmer. "Every one of you would drink twice what you could pay for. Then I'd have to pack you out of here to boot."

"But why do you have to close down the bar?" grumbled another.

"'Cause I can't keep bar and doctor at the same time," he said as he led Carter, Abe, and the marshal into a side room. "I need my table, gentlemen," he said to four, well-dressed men playing poker.

"Oh, let 'em continue," muttered the marshal. "You can wrap up this guy's hand while he's sittin' in your barber chair. Besides, I want him sittin' up where I can see his eyes when I ask him questions. Eyes always—and I mean always—tell me when a man's lyin'. You get that, kid?"

"Yes, sir," Abe said. "I've got no reason to tell you anything but the truth."

"We'll see. Sit there."

"Be careful, now," said Gilmer. "Don't let your hand get over my chair. I paid twenty-six bucks for that chair. Had it shipped from Chicago, and I don't want no blood on it."

Abe sat down and looked at his hand. It was hurting something awful now and shaking so he couldn't hold it still. Gilmer brought a lamp over and a basin to catch the blood that was still dripping like a clock ticking.

"Well . . . looks like you got a graze cuttin' right across the back of your hand. Can you move your fingers?" Abe tried, and could do so, in spite of the pain. "You're mighty lucky, son. You'll have a nasty scar, and probably some stiffness. But you're lucky. A little deeper, and it would have cut those tendons . . . that, or crushed the bones. Then you'd've had nothin' but a club for a hand."

As Gilmer worked to stop the bleeding and wrap up Abe's hand, the marshal fired a dozen questions at Abe, occasionally looking over to Carter for verification. "You say you left two friends back eatin' dinner? What're you three doin' in Newton, anyway?"

"I already told you; we're here looking for land to start a colony on."

"I don't understand this colony business. Say, Sid," the marshal said, turning to one of the men at the table, "do me a favor and see if you can find those two. I want 'em in here."

When Sid returned, he not only brought Noah and Jonas, but a third man, also dressed in plain black—obviously Matthew Keim.

"You all know this boy?" asked the marshal.

"Yes, we do," answered Jonas. "He's with us." Noah nodded his head. Both men were looking at Abe with wide, confused eyes.

"Humph," the marshal grunted, looking the three men up and down. "You could never tell by looking at you. What's that, some kinda uniform?"

"What happened?" asked Keim soberly.

"Well," said the marshal, "if he's telling the truth—and I'm inclined to believe he is at this point, if that's agreeable to you, Mr. Carter . . ."

Carter nodded his head.

"Seems as though your boy attempted a mighty brave thing. Mr. Carter was walking out behind the Silver Spoon, here, when he got jumped by someone—probably a drifter. He was knocked over the head and went down cold. Apparently, your Miller came up as the thief was going through Mr. Carter's pockets taking his money and watch. According to Miller, he got Mr. Carter's gun and tried to stop the thief. But I guess that snake shot first, and grazed the boy's hand." He turned to Abe. "Too bad you weren't a little faster, Miller, and plugged him right between the eyes. We got too many of his kind."

"You say he drew a gun on a man?" asked Keim. He and Noah and Jonas were staring at Abe in disbelief.

"It wasn't his gun. But somehow he got Mr. Carter's pistol out of his holster and was fixin' to use it."

"But that can't be right!" exclaimed Keim. "We—the four of us—are Mennonites and do not believe in violence of any kind. We would never take up a weapon against another man. It's part of our faith. Nobody can be in our church who would do a thing like that."

The marshal's eyebrows went up. "Is that true?" he asked Noah and Jonas.

The two men nodded their heads but looked bewildered.

"Well, now, that does create a problem," said the marshal, a grin spreading over his face. "What do you say to that, Miller? Sounds like there's a rather big hole in your alibi." The man leaned close, right in Abe's face. "Either you did as you said, in which case these men are ready to disown you. Or you're with them, in which case they say you couldn't have done as you claim. So." The marshal straightened up. "You're either the hero . . . or the prime suspect in this case. What'll it be?"

Abe swallowed. "But I didn't shoot anybody! There was only one shot fired . . . and I'm the one with the wounded hand."

"That may be true," said the marshal. "But nobody else saw the third man, either. It would be quite a trick, but you could've knocked Mr. Carter over the head, stole his money and watch, stashed 'em somewhere, then shot your own hand to make it look like there was a third person."

This was getting ridiculous, Abe thought. "Now, why would I do that?"

"I admit it would be crazy. But I tell you, since I been mar-shalling, I've seen more crazies than you can shake a stick at. As for why you might do such a thing, that's easy. If we would have bought your story, you'd have been beyond suspicion."

"Hold it," said Carter. "There's one easy way to check. If he shot himself with my gun, there'd be an empty chamber. Even if he reloaded quickly, you could smell it. I haven't fired my gun since last fall when I shot a rattler."

Gilmer pulled the gun out of his belt and smelled it. "It's clean," he said without hesitation and handed it to the marshal. The marshal took a sniff and nodded his head. Abe sighed with relief.

"Well, like it or not, looks like your boy's got some backbone in him," the marshal said to the three men in plain garb. Then he turned to Abe. "Lemme give you some advice, son. If you're gonna nose around places in the dark in this town, you better pack a gun. Now . . . get on out of here. We got work to do tryin' to track down that drifter."

Outside in the street, Keim spoke first. "Brothers, this is serious. We're new in these parts, and everyone knows whatever we do. To have one of the first Mennonites on the scene take up a gun shames our witness."

Abe looked down and scuffed his toe in the dirt. He didn't know what to say. He never meant to grab that gun; he didn't know what caused him to do it. Everything was such a jumble. Ever since the death of his family, it seemed like the tornado had sucked something out of him . . . maybe it had sucked the *good* out of him, made him crazy.

"You're pretty young to be on a mission like this, anyway," Keim said, frowning at Abe. "Showalter, Eby . . . how'd you pick this man to make the trip with you?"

"We didn't," volunteered Jonas. "We only just met in Council Bluffs."

"You didn't know him? Well, in that case," Keim argued, "how do we know he's one of the brethren? Wearin' plain clothes doesn't necessarily make one a brother in good standing."

"That's enough!" Jonas interrupted. "Elder Brenneman sent

him." And then Jonas went on to make a long statement in firm, passionate German.

"Yes, but Jonas," Keim protested, "it's more than the witness of the church. I know God can forgive, but this situation also creates extra danger for those who may come after. This is a very violent land out here, and the only way our people will be safe is if everyone knows that we will not respond in kind . . . no matter what the provocation."

"You think wrong, Brother Keim. The way of peace is never safe, and it is a great deception to think so. Remember, 'Straight is the gate, and narrow is the way, which leadeth unto life.'"

"I'm just sayin' that . . ."

Abe didn't listen to what Keim had to say. He knew he couldn't keep his problems to himself any longer. Sooner or later they'd pop out again like they had out in the alley— maybe with worse consequences. It wasn't fair to burden these men with that. They had a colony to establish. He had a score to settle—but with whom? Bauder? Himself? God? Abe wasn't sure, but he had to find out.

"Uh, listen," he broke in. "I appreciate what you're tryin' to do for me, Jonas, but I think Keim has a point. I probably shouldn't be on this survey. I got somethin' I need to work out, and I think I'd better be on my way."

"Now that's not necessary, son."

"Yeah, but I've made up my mind. I want to take my leave."

"But . . . where'll you be goin'?" asked Noah. "Back home?"

"I don't know . . . maybe." But what's back there for me? Abe wondered to himself. There'd be many folks who wouldn't welcome him anymore than Keim if they heard he'd picked up a gun. He might be able to keep his thoughts to himself, but he couldn't hide his hand. There'd be questions . . .

"Well, you know you belong with us, with your people," said Jonas gravely. "But if you've got somethin' to do, well, maybe the survey team isn't the best place."

The four talked on, making plans. Jonas wanted to be sure Abe had enough money. Abe assured him that he had several gold coins under a false bottom in his leather case. Finally the men shook hands and separated. Jonas and Noah went with Matthew Keim to begin a moonlight ride north to his place in the country. Abe got his bag and headed for a hotel in Newton.

Tomorrow he'd figure out what to do. Maybe he wouldn't go home. Maybe he'd go west . . . to Oregon, and face this thing head on.

Chapter 7

"You the one who drew on Red River Cob last night?" Abe took another bite of buckwheat cakes with chokecherry syrup. He washed it down with coffee and looked up at the one-legged cook who was trying to put another stick of wood into his black stove. "I don't know any Red River Cob."

"Well, I figured you was the one who tried to stop him robbin' Carter last night, 'cause of your hand. Was ya?"

"Oh, that . . . yeah, I guess. But who's Cob?"

"That's right—you ain't from around these parts, are ya? Well, Cob's the drifter who lifted Carter's money." The cook slammed the door on his stove and turned the damper. He yelped and swore as he jerked back and spun around on his crutch. "That baby's hot. Gotta be careful, or I'm liable to burn down the ol' Succulent Bivouac."

Abe looked around the inside of the dirty little tent. Boards on sawhorses made the table from which he ate. His three-legged stool was about to give way, and the dirt floor hadn't been swept of the food that had fallen the day before.

Ah. The Succulent Bivouac, thought Abe; yes, that *had* been the name painted on the board above the flap outside. He should have guessed what to expect from the name, but the food was good. He marveled at how the cook kept his crutch under his arm without ever adjusting its position. Both hands were free, and he moved as fast as any two-legged man.

"They caught Cob last night, just afore midnight, ya know," the cook said as he stirred up some more batter. "If you was to ask me, marshal's mighty lucky, too. That Cob's a cagey one. You'd expect most hombres to light a shuck for parts unknown after knocking off somebody like that. But not ol' Cob. Cool as can be, he just curled up in the hayloft over Horner's stable. Old Jeb woulda rounded up a posse and been to Topeka and back by now if it weren't for that luck o' his."

"What luck's that?"

"His good luck, Cob's bad luck. Works both ways, I 'spose. What gave him away was countin' the money. So happens he dropped a fifty-dollar gold piece. Skittered right down through the straw. And wouldn't ya know it, but it found a crack in the loft boards and fell straight through. Well, directly, the marshal comes in to get his horse what was in the stall below . . . Say, haven't you heard all this already?"

"Not a word of it," said Abe.

"Hmm. Well, I ain't funnin' you none, but right there in the light of his dim ol' lantern, Jeb spies a shiny gold piece stickin' pretty as you please right out of the top of a pile of dung! Now he knowed it's been costin' him a lot to feed that horse of his, but this is the first time he got any return . . . Heh-heh-heh!"

The cook wheezed with laughter at his own joke. "Heh-heh . . . When Jeb leans down to pick it up, however, he took to thinkin' 'bout the way it was stickin' up there. And then it comes to him that it probably dropped from above . . . So, out backs Jeb and fetches some help. And that's how they caught Cob."

"Hmm," murmured Abe, drinking the last of his coffee. "Did Mr. Carter get all his money back?"

"So they say."

"How long you been in Newton?"

"Ever since the tracks got laid through here. But I'm aimin' to move on down to Wichita. More business there."

"How far west does the train go?"

"Some day a body'll be able to go all the way to 'Frisco if he don't mind a-ziggin' and a-zaggin' some. They're almost finished with the line through to the border. Saw a bunch of railroad officials in here the other day. They's fixin' a powerful big shindig for when they win that land grant."

"Could a guy get through to Pueblo now?"

"Not by train. There's sometimes a stage that shuttles 'tween the construction site and Pueblo, but it ain't very dependable. Course a feller could always take Shank's mares."

"What?"

"*Walk* . . . heh-heh . . . ya know, from where it ain't finished. You could make it in a couple days. Maybe you could rent a horse, or maybe they even got wagons goin' back and forth haulin' stuff. I dunno."

Abe paid for his breakfast and went out. Going west—if that's what he decided to do—wasn't going to be as easy as catching the next train. He walked aimlessly out of town toward the stock pens. He wasn't sure he should go west, but something drew him . . . or maybe it was that nothing drew him home to Goshen. It didn't even feel like home to him anymore—just someplace in his distant past. No family . . . the farm needing rebuilding . . . and how would he tell his friends at church what had happened, why he was coming back early? He supposed he'd have to explain someday, but not now. First he needed to . . . to . . . the riptides shifted within him.

Back at the station, he discovered the next train west wouldn't be through till evening. But the one going east was due in thirty minutes. East . . . west . . . What difference did it make? Going west had been nothing more than a foolish notion anyway. Abe bought a ticket for home and sat in the cold December sun to wait.

Later in the morning as his train coach swayed along over the Kansas prairie, back toward Topeka, he dug through his bag and pulled out the newspaper. There were more items to read, he told himself as he looked them over, but his eyes kept going back to the story about the "Modoc War."

Even if he could have gone straight west from Newton, there was no way of catching Mary; she was too far ahead of him. He wished he could be sure her father would protect her. But thoughts about Bauder only made Abe more nervous. A man who would use blackmail to get his way, even if it started a war and risked the lives of other people, couldn't be trusted to think about anyone else.

I wonder if there is a way I could stop Bauder? Abe mused. Maybe the way to stop Bauder was at the point of his success in getting the Indians pushed off his place. Morally, he just seemed like a greedy land grabber. But Mary had mentioned something more: blackmail. And that was a crime. Abe's mind was racing. He was getting an idea.

The key was the blackmail.

Other than Mary and Bauder and that guy in Washington, no one else but me knows that Odeneal shouldn't be the Indian superintendent, thought Abe. Odeneal had his position because of a crime—Bauder's blackmail. If he could inform the right people of Bauder's manipulation, they might arrange to disqualify Odeneal and reinstate Meacham. And if Meacham got his old position back, he would certainly do what he could to stop the war and negotiate peace with the Modocs.

Abe looked up from the paper. How could he accomplish such a maneuver? It was crazy even dreaming of it . . . and yet, if there was a way, it might save Mary and . . . and avert more bloodshed. But who could help him? To begin with, who would believe him?

Davis. Jonathan Davis would believe him, the one person he could trust. If there was a way to pull off the plan, the little man with the walrus mustache might know how.

Davis had said he was going to Denver. Colorado was on the way west, anyhow. Abe tried to remember train maps he had seen hanging on station walls. He was pretty sure that one train went all the way west across Kansas. And if the one he was on wasn't yet completed through to Colorado, then there had to be another.

He asked the next conductor who came through his car.

"Yep. The Kansas Pacific," came the answer.

"Well, where and when can I make connections?"

"Topeka. But I don't know the time. I only work on the Santa Fe here. Those monkeys up there keep changin' the schedule. Never can depend on them."

Topeka, Kansas, was the supper stop for the evening, but Abe didn't follow the crowd to the restaurant. Instead, he found the station agent who was wrestling with some boxes on the platform. He was a little man, working without a jacket. Suspenders crossed the back of his smudged, white shirt. "Say, big boy, can you give me a hand here? I need to get these under cover before it rains tonight."

"Sure, I'll help ya. But could you tell me when's the next train to Denver?"

"Sittin' on that track there, the other side of the station. Leaves in . . .," he pulled out his watch, "exactly three minutes. Here, grab the other side of that box."

Abe grabbed. "How much?"

"Oh, I'd guess about eighty pounds."

"No. I mean the ticket to Denver. How much does it cost?"

"Twenty-eight, sixty."

"I'd like a ticket," Abe grunted as he hefted most of the weight.

"Well, you're going to have to hurry." A whistle sounded to emphasize the agent's warning.

"I know, but you gotta sell me the ticket."

"I will . . . uh! Just this one more crate."

In exasperation, Abe picked up the crate by himself and hurried into the station. "Now, can I have my ticket?"

"Sure." The man went behind his window.

"How 'bout this other ticket going east? I only used part of it.

Can I get some money back?"

"Sure thing. Here's your change and your ticket for Denver. Now let me see that other ticket."

Abe handed it to him and looked up just in time to see the Denver train start to pull away. He forgot the refund, grabbed his bag, and ran out the door. He just made the step of the last car.

For thirty-six hours Abe jostled across Kansas and into Colorado in the discomfort of the train coach. The air seemed stale; often smoke from the engine filtered in. The coach was too hot when the stove was stoked, but it was a small heater and burned the soft cottonwood rapidly. Soon, the winter chill crept in again. Cramped space, strange food, and very little sleep and exercise was beginning to make Abe feel sick. He'd never imagined a country could be so big. His half-asleep dreams were filled with panicky starts that he had slept through the Denver stop and was nearly to the Pacific Ocean.

When the first thin light of morning began to chase away the night, Abe was awake, staring out the window. It was December 8 . . . how long had he been traveling? In the far distance a bank of clouds lining the horizon began to take on jagged shapes. It looked like a wild storm was brewing. The dawn began to tinge the tops with an eerie pink.

"Red sky at night, sailor's delight . . . Red sky in the morning, sailor's warning," Abe muttered to himself, then smiled. Where had he ever learned that saying? There'd never been any sea-going people in his family. In fact, he didn't think he'd ever met a sailor.

Then Abe sat up with a start. Those weren't clouds the sun was painting red. They were mountains . . . mountains with snow halfway down them. As the morning broke, he could see that they extended as far south and north as a person could see. He'd never seen anything like them. Nobody back home would believe him if he tried to tell them how big they were.

The more he watched the horizon, the more mesmerized

he became. The mountains growing in size made him feel like he was on the brink of something new. So far his travels had had a strange effect on him. The huge size of the country amazed him, but somehow, though he'd come across rivers and plains and prairies, from green fields to deserts, he'd felt let down, dissatisfied. It wasn't so much a disappointment in the scenery—he'd had few expectations. But with every mile clicking away beneath the wheels of the train, he'd felt more depressed . . . a melancholy about life, a frustration that it didn't hold more for him.

Suddenly, the mountains seemed to be shouting: There is more! Just by being there they beckoned him . . . not merely to climb them or cross them, but assuring him that there was more to life than an endless rolling sameness. They stirred a new feeling inside him: excitement, hope.

Abe stretched and sat up straight in his seat. He would find Davis . . . and maybe go on to Oregon to find Mary, too.

Chapter 8

*A*s the train rolled into Denver, Abe realized that it wouldn't be so easy to find Davis. He'd imagined Denver a small, sleepy village. But it was obviously a rapidly growing city with many new buildings of unweathered wood, and numerous brick structures, too.

At the station, he approached two men who were off-loading a cord of wood from their wagon for the train.

"Could you tell me where the hotels are?"

One pointed over his shoulder with his thumb. "This street here, you can go either way and find one."

"Are there any others?"

"How many does one man need?"

Abe laughed with them. "No. I'm looking for someone who's staying here in Denver, but I don't know where to start."

The men told Abe where other hotels were, and Abe began his search. By noon he'd made his rounds to each one and felt like he'd worn his legs off. No one had a Jonathan Davis registered or had ever heard of him.

Abe began to feel desperate and started asking everyone he passed on the street. Most people were friendly and tried to be helpful, considering for a moment whether they had seen a new man in town fitting Davis' description. A few were irritated at being interrupted. But no one could remember Davis.

Discouraged, he sat on a bench in front of the assay office. The office was closed, and in a few minutes he realized why. Across the street and down a ways, the doors to a whitewashed church opened, and people started filing out.

It was Sunday, and Abe hadn't even remembered.

He felt guilty and confused. What was he doing out here a thousand miles from home? Chasing will-o'-the-wisps and forgetting God more each day, that's what. He remembered how often his father used to quote, "Seek ye first the kingdom of God and his righteousness." Guess I haven't been doing much of that lately, thought Abe.

A well-dressed man and woman came from the church and got into an expensive buggy parked at the rail in front of Abe. The man wore new-looking boots and a fine western hat.

"Excuse me," Abe said as he stood up. "You wouldn't happen to be a cattleman by any chance, would you?"

"As a matter of fact, I do run a few thousand head just west of here," the man said, taking up the reins. "What can I do for you?"

"I'm lookin' for a man named Jonathan Davis . . . short fellow, bald head, large mustache?"

"Sorry . . . don't know the man."

"This man is just passin' through. He's a salesman for barb-wire."

"Oh, *him*. Had no use for his wire. This is open range around here. First person to put up wire would get burned out." The rancher gee-upped to his horses.

"Hey, wait! You know where I can find him?" Abe ran after the buggy a few steps.

"Try May Bell's," came the faint words from the dust and clattering of the buggy.

When Abe finally found it, May Bell's was a small boarding house in the older part of town. The boarders were just sitting down to Sunday dinner, and Abe realized how hungry he was—having had nothing to eat since the night before. But as he looked around the table, his heart sank. There was no Jonathan Davis.

"Mr. Davis is staying here," assured May, the proprietress. "I do expect him directly . . . just late from church, I imagine. If you've a mind, you can take a seat over there and wait."

The boarders ignored him as they continued their meal.

Davis in church? Abe wouldn't have guessed it. Davis was a traveling salesman, far from home, with no one to impress. Maybe there was more to him than Abe had noticed.

When Davis walked in, he stopped in shock. "Miller! What are you doing here? I thought you'd be plowing up Kansas by now."

"Well, some problems came up . . . and I wasn't needed there anymore. So, I just decided to take a trip."

"Ha! Going after that gal in Oregon, aren't ya?"

"Oh, no . . . no. I wouldn't dream of bothering her none," Abe stammered. "Though . . . well, I guess I'd like to see her . . . mostly just concerned about her safety."

Davis grinned. "That's what it's all about, kid, startin' to care about someone else's welfare." He slapped Abe on the back. "I knew you'd been bit back there on the train . . . Say, May, got some vittles for this man?"

"No, Mr. Davis. You know the house rules. You gotta tell me and *pay* me a day in advance for any meal guests."

"But I couldn't tell you! I didn't know he was comin'."

"And I couldn't prepare. There's barely enough for the regulars. You all eat like horses. So he can just go on down to the cantina if he's hungry. And as for you, you'd better get over here if you want anything at all."

"Forget it, May. Come on, Abe . . . let's go." Davis put on his bowler hat and headed for the door. "They got the best chili con carne you've ever eaten—made with buffalo."

In a back corner of a little cafe, Davis sat pulling at his big walrus mustache. "Hey, what happened to your hand?" he asked, pointing to the now dirty bandage that Abe still wore.

"It's nothin'," Abe said as he looked at his hand, turning it from front to back and making a fist to demonstrate that it had recovered.

"But how 'bout Kansas. Did you Mennonite fellers give up

on breakin' new ground?"

Abe told him about the robbery, how he'd pulled Carter's gun, and the effect it'd had on the Mennonite brothers. He left nothing out. "I don't know quite why I did it," Abe said. "It just seemed like I had to stop that guy! But when I think about actually shooting someone, I can't even believe what I did."

Abe shrugged. "Afterward, I was gonna head home to Goshen, but I'd have to tell people there. What would they say? What could I say? I don't know why I did it, and I don't know what I'd do if I faced the same thing again. It's like I don't trust myself anymore."

"Well, that's what comes of trustin' in yourself."

Abe was startled. "What do ya mean?"

"Listen, Miller. I don't quite see eye to eye with you people about turnin' the other cheek and all. I believe the good Lord meant us to be forgivin' and all that, and I sure don't go around pickin' fights, but whether we should never defend ourselves or not, I'm not so sure. But . . . hey, listen. I don't want to criticize your convictions or nothin', so let's forget it."

"No, no. Go ahead. I'm interested. What did you mean about not trustin' in yourself?"

"Well . . . it's right to believe, to not be wishy-washy about your convictions. I'm all for that. But a feller can get into a heap of trouble if he starts buildin' an image about how he's *gonna* act when the time comes. That's all I mean about trustin' in yourself. And I should know . . . I lost my family that way— trustin' in myself, I mean."

"I didn't know you had a family."

"Well, I don't no more. But . . . that's another story."

"What happened to them?" Abe pressed.

"Look. It's just that I thought I was beyond getting involved with another woman. But when the opportunity came . . . well, I wasn't above it. 'Nuff said?"

Abe sat in silence eating his chili. He hardly noticed the spices burning his mouth. There was so much more he had to learn about himself.

"Hey. I didn't mean to rain on your parade!" Davis said, giving Abe a playful shove. "Come on. Tell me where you're headed. How'd you happen to come to Denver? I still think you're headed out to see that girl."

"Actually, I came here to find you. I've got an idea I wanted to ask you about. There may be a way to stop that war."

"War? What war? I don't know nothin' 'bout no war."

Abe stared at Davis. Well, of course. What'd he expect—for Davis to be a mind reader? He took a big breath.

"Well, you remember when Bauder hit Mary on the train?" Davis nodded.

"Well, he hit her 'cause she accused him of blackmail. And I heard enough to know that's exactly what it was." Abe dug out the newspaper and shoved it toward Davis. "Here, read this," he said, pointing to the story about the Modocs.

Davis held it up to catch the light coming in through the front window. After a few minutes, he said, "Sounds like things are really poppin' a cork out there. But what's this idea of yours you think is gonna stop the fighting?"

Abe relayed the story of how Bauder had threatened the Washington official with exposure of his squaw wife unless he arranged to replace Superintendent Meacham with Odeneal. "So you see, this Odeneal is really Bauder's man to drive the Indians off his range, and if it takes the army and a war to do it, he couldn't care less. I figure that if I can send a wire to the Indian Bureau in Washington about what happened, the people there will most likely reverse this appointment and reinstate Meacham. Then there'd be a chance for Meacham to stop the war. But . . . I can't pull this off by myself. You're the only other person who witnessed the kind of man Bauder is. If there's two of us giving the same story, someone just might believe us. That's . . . that's why I came here to Denver—to get you to help me. I figured that with all the travelin' you do, you'd know how to do it."

Abe stopped to let Davis consider his plan, but he knew it would work. It had to! Abe would do more than just rescue Mary; he would stop the blasted war. That would show Bauder that his blackmail and bully ways didn't pay . . . and there'd probably be some penalty for Bauder interfering with the proper function of the United States Government.

Davis sat pulling on his mustache. "It won't work, Abe. You and me, we're nobodies sittin' out here in the middle of the wilderness as far as those bureaucrats in D.C. are concerned. Why would they believe this wild story you've got about what you heard on the train concerning what's happening in Oregon? See? It gets pretty far-fetched."

Davis leaned forward. "In fact, there's only one person in Washington who'd believe you . . . and that's the guy Bauder blackmailed. We don't even know his name, but if by some chance he got holda' your wire, he'd believe you, all right . . . and burn it as fast as greased lightnin'. *That* you can count on."

Abe felt crushed. Davis was right. There was no way to convince the right people in Washington. But . . . he couldn't just give up. He had a valid point: Bauder *had* committed a crime, and if justice could be restored, peace might also be restored. There had to be another way.

"What if I sent a message to Meacham in Oregon? He could inform the army commander there and possibly get things straightened out."

"That might work," conceded Davis. "But your message could still fall into the wrong hands—the settlers, Odeneal, even Bauder himself. There's probably a lot of people out there who would quietly lose such a telegram before it reached Meacham. And you don't even know where to find Meacham . . . what town he lives in, I mean."

Abe threw up his hands. "Then what can I do?"

Davis shrugged. "I don't think there is any way . . . from here. You'd have to deliver the information yourself to be sure it got to the right people."

Abe thought for a few minutes, his mouth setting in a hard line. "Then that's what I'm gonna do."

"Now, wait a minute!" Davis protested. "I wasn't suggestin' you go. That'd be a fool thing to do. If Bauder got wind of the story you're trying to peddle, your life would be worth less than an Injun's."

"Yeah. But like you said, it might work. Right?"

"Well, it might . . . if Meacham believed you. But . . ."

"And he's the most likely person to believe me. Don't forget he lost his job, probably without any explanation. I'm sure he knows what Bauder's after. And by now it's obvious what Odeneal is deliverin'."

"Well, yeah. But it'd be a risky thing to try alone.

"Can I get out there by train?"

"Sure. Just go up to Cheyenne, then west on the Transcontinental. But it goes to California, not Oregon."

"Well, there's got to be a way, 'cause that's the train Bauder and Mary were on . . . Say. How 'bout you comin' with me?" Abe asked. "You said it'd be risky to try alone, but with someone vouchin' for my story, I'd have a better chance."

Davis smiled. "Gee, Abe. I'd love to. You know what I think about Oregon. But . . . I got to head over to Leadville tomorrow. I got a sure sale there, and business hasn't been goin' so well lately. I gotta make a buck."

"There's cattle ranchers out in Oregon who might buy some wire."

"I don't know. The problem is that I'm already too far west. It's all open range around here. The only fences are holdin' pens and corrals. And, where there's lots of trees, a man can easily make fences from rails." Davis hesitated, turned and looked out the window. "It sure would be nice, though. You tempt me, Abe. You really tempt me."

The two men sat silently for a few minutes, each thinking.

"How do you think I oughtta go about tellin' Meacham . . . once I find him?"

"First, you gotta find someone to cover your backside."

"My what?"

"Your backside . . . you know, someone you can trust in case Bauder catches wind of what your . . . oh, Abe. Listen. Tell you what I'll do. After I make this deal in Leadville, I'll come with you. Okay?"

"When'll that be?"

"Couple days at the most. Not long."

"I don't know. I think time's critical. I'd like to get on the road today."

"But I gotta finish this deal."

"What if you followed me . . . you know, as soon as you're finished?"

"I 'spose I could do that."

"Good." Abe grinned. "It's a deal then."

On the way back to the train station, Abe tried to remember the town near the Bauder ranch Mary had mentioned. Link . . . Link-something.

"That'd be Linkville, Oregon," said the ticket agent, spreading out a map and a schedule sheet. "Looks like you'd have to change trains in Rocklin, California, then head on up the valley to Red Bluff. From there, I guess you'd probably have to catch a stage the rest of the way."

"That's likely to take several days," moaned Abe.

"There's a shorter way if you're in a hurry," said a strange voice.

Abe turned around to see the skinniest man he'd ever seen, leaning against a support post of the station. The man wore fringed buckskins—old, stained, and worn shiny where they weren't worn through. A twelve-inch bowie knife with a horn handle hung from his belt directly in front, and his hair and beard were so long and matted they looked like a hair ball some cat had spit up.

"Ya did say you wanted to get to Linkville, didn't ya?"

"Well, yes sir. That's where I'm headin'."

The man had uncommon eyes . . . a blue so light that they almost looked white. If it wasn't for the black line that circled the iris, a person might think there was none—only black pupils in the middle of an all-white ball. The man took advantage of their impact on others by staring coolly at them until they looked away first.

When Abe glanced back, there was a hint of a grin at the corners of the mountain man's mouth. "And you be wantin' to get there sooner rather than later, don't ya?"

"That's right. Do you know a way?"

The man nodded. "It's called the Applegate trail. Been over it a dozen times . . . cheaper too. Get off the train at Winnemucca, Nevada. Folks there'll tell you the way."

"How much would I save?" Abe asked the agent.

"Now I wouldn't advise that," said the train agent.

"How much?"

"'Bout seven bucks. But this is winter, man, and there's no tellin' what you'd run into, even if there is such a trail."

"Oh, there's a trail all right, and a pretty good one, too," assured the mountain man. "Scores of wagons have gone over it."

"But this young man's not familiar with the country."

"I ain't pushin' him," the man shrugged. "I just mentioned a shorter way. That's all."

"Thank you, Mister. I think I'll try it," Abe said. He turned back to the agent. "Give me a ticket to Winnemucca."

The ticket agent shook his head. "All right, son. But don't say I recommended it. I think you're headin' for trouble."

Chapter 9

*T*hree evenings later, Abe got off the train in Winnemucca, Nevada. He was bone tired and hungry. The regular meal stop was on down the track at Humboldt, but he'd had enough of railroad food. Ever since the beautiful dining room in Cheyenne with its fine linen and crystal, the railroad houses had gone downhill. Some had been little better than crude shanties by the tracks, trying to pass off prairie dogs as a new variety of chicken.

No more of that for him. He'd find a restaurant or saloon in Winnemucca that would serve a good meal.

As he entered the station, Abe noticed an old man standing inside. "Howdy," Abe said, trying to be friendly in the western way he had noticed ever since Kansas. He figured that in this wild land with so few people, it'd be good to make friends whenever possible.

The old-timer smiled and nodded twice in an exaggerated fashion. "By the way," Abe continued, wanting to strike up more of a conversation, "does the Applegate Trail take off from here?"

The man shook his head and frowned, again with great exaggeration. Abe started. Was it an eccentric mannerism to indicate that the trail didn't start right there at the station, or did that pronounced frown and turned down lip mean the trail was nowhere around there? Why didn't the old guy say something?

"Well, where is it then?" Abe pressed.

The old man motioned with his thumb on down the track.

"But where? Where does it start from?"

There was just another shake of the old head.

"What do you mean? Surely, you know." From outside, the whistle blew. Abe glanced through the window at the train, then dropped his bag and grabbed the man by his shoulders, "Hurry up, now; tell me where it starts, old man. I gotta know!"

But the man still refused to talk. In desperation Abe shook him, then shook again so hard that the gray head whipped back and forth. The old man snapped open his mouth as wide as a snake's. Abe let go and dropped back in horror. The man's tongue was missing.

The door slammed behind them. "Injuns got it when he was a kid," the train agent said. "Whatcha need?"

"I . . . I'm sorry," Abe stammered as he picked up his bag and turned quickly to the agent. "I need to know where the Applegate Trail starts."

The first blast of steam blew from the engine outside, then three more in rapid succession as the wheels spun and the train crept forward.

"Applegate? Takes off from Lassen's Meadows, 'bout forty miles south of here at Humboldt."

Abe caught the train on the run and rode for two more miserable hours. Why did that old mountain man in Denver tell me to get off at Winnemucca? he fumed. Forty extra miles by horse would have added nearly a whole day to his trip, and that old guy knew he was pressed for time.

By the time he got to Humboldt, Abe didn't care much where or what he ate. But the rail house food wasn't bad. For seventy-five cents he got three mountain trout, hot biscuits with butter and jam, and all the sauerkraut he could eat.

Where Winnemucca had been a town of about a thousand, Humbolt had only twenty-eight people. There wasn't a real livery, just a man, Jake Potter, who stabled a few horses to let. Abe had to roust him out of his house. "We don't run no all-night show here, ya know," the man grumbled. "Why don't you come back in the morning?"

"I'm sorry," said Abe, "but I want to get an early start."

But when Abe told him he was heading out the Applegate Trail, Potter wouldn't rent him a horse. Abe assured him that he'd grown up with horses and knew how to take proper care of an animal. "And I'll be back in no more than two or three weeks," he promised.

"And if you don't, I'm out a horse," Potter growled. "You want a horse, you buy it. If ya come back, and the horse is in good shape, I'll give ya what's fair fer it. But I won't rent no horse to a greenhorn headin' off into the Black Rock Desert. The horse may find his way back, but by then you could have ruined it in that desert."

"But this is winter," protested Abe. "The desert shouldn't be any problem this time of year."

"See? That's just what I mean. You don't have any idea what you're headin' into. You might be a strappin' strong lad who knows horses, but you'll get whittled down to size pretty quick out there, and I don't aim to lose a horse in the process. The desert in the winter can be as mean as under the blazin' sun. You jes remember that."

Abe hadn't figured on having to buy a horse with his small store of gold coins, but he had no choice. He chose a tough-looking roan, then exchanged his travel bag for a saddle and blanket. Potter said he was used to outfitting prospectors and had plenty of jerky and hard biscuits if Abe wanted them. As Abe was paying, the liveryman said, "Say, I got a buffalo coat and a rifle I'll let you have at a good price. You'll be needin' both if that's all the clothes you got."

Abe considered his money. His Mennonite clothes were warm, but they wouldn't do for spending long hours in wind and bad weather. And he might have to shoot some game for food along the way. He took the coat and rifle, and stuffed the few remaining gold pieces in his pocket. He'd have to figure out how to get his train fare for home later—maybe he could work for a few days or something.

In spite of complaining about being roused out of bed, Potter was a talker and eager to tell Abe about the desert. He'd been across it several times himself and knew all the tales about the explorers and the wagon trains that had followed them.

At first light next morning, Abe rode out under a low-hanging gray sky. A couple inches of old snow covered the ground, but he had no trouble finding the trail where it left Lassen's Meadows and forded the Humboldt River. The wagon tracks of the many settlers were clear as they struck west across the low range of mountains. "Those'll be the Antelopes," Potter had said.

It surprised Abe to see dozens of derelict, weathered wagons, bedsteads, and once-beautiful breakfronts and dressers scattered along the trail. The grade seemed easy, and he was only a few hours out from town. Why had the pioneers abandoned so many belongings so soon?

Then, among the junk, he began to notice the bones of oxen and horses. At first they had looked so nearly like the white snow that he hadn't seen them, but when he began to count, he soon tallied over fifty skeletons in no more than a few miles. The land was desert at this point. Even back at Lassen's Meadows, there hadn't been enough graze for even a small herd, in Abe's opinion.

That must have been the reason for leaving all the stuff behind, thought Abe. These settlers had already come over seventeen hundred miles. Their wagons were worn out, their stock weak and exhausted. The people themselves were making an all-out, last-ditch effort to get to the promised land. It was life or death. Anything that hindered them had to go.

Abe had read about the great migration. In their final desperation, many wayfarers had loaded the barest of essentials onto their own backs and had set out to finish the journey on foot, keeping themselves alive on occasion by carving half-rotten steaks from the carcasses along the way. Occasionally, Abe noticed a cross by the trail with a simple name carved into it and sometimes a date.

By noon, the sky was spitting snow, and Abe was glad for the buffalo coat as he pulled the collar up around his neck.

Within another hour, he came to the first water hole Potter had told him to expect. At least he hoped he was at the right spot. It was a miserable water hole—brackish and shallow. Even the occasional tufts of stiff, thick grass grew away from the water's edge as though trying to avoid some poison. Abe was sure he wasn't going to drink any of the vile stuff, and he didn't know whether he should let his horse have any. Then he noticed some tracks. They looked like dog tracks—probably coyote, he thought. They ran down to the water's edge through the mud as though the animal had come there to drink. Maybe it was okay.

He let his horse drink, but the condition of the water continued to worry him. Certainly, such a foul puddle wasn't the kind of place people marked on maps or told others about. Was he at the right spot? So far, he'd been following a clear trail. From time to time as he wound through the desert hills, he still saw the remains of wagons and fallen oxen. But it was possible that the trail had divided, and he had taken the wrong fork.

He looked again at the little mud puddle. That might not even be a spring, he thought. Maybe there was a rain recently, and that's just run off. Even the mud around the edge was white with alkali.

Abe walked around while he ate some jerked beef and a couple biscuits and drank the last of the water from his canteen. When he got north of the water hole, he smelled something dead. He followed the scent until he found a dead antelope under some sage brush about thirty yards away. He went back quickly to his horse. The horse was leaning down for a second drink. Abe yanked him up just in time. Maybe it was the water that had gotten the antelope, maybe something else, but he didn't want to take any chances—not out in this wilderness.

Abe pressed on, riding hard. The livery man had said that if he made good time, he could come out of the hills onto the edge of the Black Rock Desert before night fall. There, he should find a better water hole—Rabbithole Spring. But as he rode, it snowed harder. For the first time Abe began to worry that he might lose the trail altogether. Even if he was on the wrong one, it had been a clear trail, and there was comfort in that. If it disappeared, he'd have to go by dead reckoning . . . when the storm let up enough for him to get his bearings.

He was tired and thirsty. He began to think about how he might have to melt snow for his evening camp. He was glad the gear he'd picked included a little coffee pot. "You'll find a hundred uses for it," Potter had said. "Besides, no one can make it on the trail without coffee."

As the afternoon wore on, his travel was on easy ground, meandering between low hills. Potter had said it would be that way. He took heart. Maybe he was on the right trail and would come to Rabbithole Spring soon. He certainly hoped so. The trail was almost indistinguishable in the failing light, and for hours now, he hadn't passed an abandoned wagon or any other indication that he was still on the old emigrant path. He tried to reassure himself: maybe he had missed the stuff now that the snow was building up a little. It was only about four inches, but it was fresh and sat atop everything, turning it into an unbroken, rippling blanket of white.

Slowly, his horse picked its way through a narrow gorge, and as Abe looked ahead, he realized that he could no longer see more than a couple hundred feet. Whether it was the snow or the failing light, there was only a featureless gray curtain ahead of him.

And then, suddenly, a large, kidney-shaped black area materialized on his right. When he got closer, he saw a couple boards tacked together to make a sign. Half-covered by snow, it said, "Rabbithole Spring."

He jumped off his horse and ran to the water, eagerly scooping up a drink. He sprayed the first mouthful out like an engine blowing steam. The water was bitter. And when he looked closer, he could see that it was dirty, too. But his horse drank it gratefully. Abe tried another swallow. His stomach wrenched. He didn't know whether it was just his anxiety or if the water was really putrid.

He looked at the sign again. No question about what it said. And then Abe noticed a broken wagon nearby. This had to be the place. He remembered the story Potter had told him how back in '46, Jesse Applegate and a dozen men had been at a loss for water after coming east across the blistering Black Rock Desert. Then they noticed trails left in the sand by rabbits. Shrewdly thinking that these would converge on water, they followed them, and thus discovered what was still known as Rabbithole Spring.

If a body's thirsty enough, thought Abe, I guess it's wet. He tried another mouthful and managed to hold it down. "Maybe coffee will taste better," he said aloud.

Abe built a fire from some boards broken off the wagon and made coffee. The heat from the fire was thin in the gusty wind. His horse drifted off a way and chomped on the stiff grass. Abe couldn't imagine how an animal could live on the stuff.

It was soon completely dark, and, as Abe chewed on some jerky, he began to think about how alone he was. No one who cared knew where he was, except maybe Jonathan Davis. And he hadn't even told Davis about his cross-country plan. This is crazy, he thought. The snow finally stopped, but the wind picked up as Abe sat staring into the fire. He thought about how comforting his family's fireplace had been at home with everyone gathered around . . . Why did that all have to end? he wondered, sliding into an overwhelming melancholy.

Finally, when the fire had burned low, he roused himself

enough to feed it, then curled up under his buffalo robe and blanket and fell into a fitful sleep.

Once during the night, he awoke when his horse snorted. The fire was no more than a slight glow, but from across the pond two green eyes reflected its light. As Abe watched, a tall shape slunk away into the sage.

Chapter 10

*T*he next morning blowing snow had erased every track he had made the night before. But though he couldn't see it, Abe assumed that the wagon trail continued down the ravine.

He took his time heating some coffee and eating biscuits. Travel would not be easy, but he determined to stay calm. The light will be better in a quarter of an hour, and maybe the wind will have lessened by then—enough so I can see where I'm going, he thought.

It was more like a half hour before he was on the back of the ready roan, swinging on down the ravine. But when he came out on the flat land, his heart sank. Potter had said that he could sight in on the great black rock twenty-one miles across the flat and head straight for the base of it. But that was impossible. Abe couldn't see a quarter of a mile. Low clouds and blowing snow created a near whiteout.

He ventured on for a few hundred yards hoping that the old wagon tracks would be visible. There was not a chance. He hated to give up, but finally he headed back toward the spring. Then he knew fear. Twenty paces back the snow already covered his horse's tracks.

He dismounted and walked ahead. He'd heard of people wandering in circles in blizzards until they dropped from exhaustion. Sometimes, their bodies were discovered within a stone's throw of shelter. This wasn't a blizzard, but the effect was the same in a place so flat and featureless. He'd ridden only a few hundred yards. It shouldn't be hard to get back, but he had to keep reminding himself that the flats were over twenty miles across. If he got going in the wrong direction . . .

A hot flash washed over him. His heart was beating in the slow, hard beats he knew as panic. He tried to take a few deep breaths and tell himself he'd be okay. The feeling would pass . . . all he had to do was calm down. He needed to think, select the wisest path, not leap into doing something he'd later regret.

Abe looked behind him. He could still see tracks going off for a ways. That was worth something. This was different than a blizzard. He could see far enough to get a bearing of sorts and hopefully travel in a straight line. If I sent the horse ahead and held his tail, thought Abe, it would give me a better perspective on my direction.

Taking a handful of tail, he gave the horse a swat. It took off so fast that Abe nearly lost hold. He had to run to keep up. And then, he noticed that the horse was not going in a straight line but was definitely veering to the left. Should he let go before they were hopelessly lost, or should he stay with his horse?

He had to stay with the horse; all his gear was on it, including the rifle and his canteen. His mind shuffled through options like they were a hand of cards—a short one at that. If worse came to worst, he could kill the horse and live off it until the storm passed. He'd even heard of people surviving a storm by crawling inside the gutted carcass of a warm animal for a few hours. But the weather wasn't that cold, he told himself. Still, he'd stay with the horse, and he wouldn't have to kill it . . . he hoped.

Then Abe tripped, and tripped again. It was sagebrush. He was stumbling over sagebrush! That meant he was off the mud flat. The horse was slowing to an easy walk, and suddenly Abe realized it was taking him back up the ravine to the spring.

Abe dropped to the ground beside the black smudge that had been his fire. Thank God, that was a close one, he thought.

When he regained his breath, he stripped the saddle off his horse and wrestled the old wagon around, turning it up on its side to create a small shelter. Then he built another fire and waited out the hours.

He was facing a new problem. If he didn't get moving soon, he wouldn't be able to get across the flat before dark. Making dry camp out in the middle of that desolation would be a dangerous venture, let alone an uncomfortable one. If the weather closed in on him again during the night, he'd be as stuck as he had been before his horse led him back.

Maybe I ought to give up this whole thing, he thought. God doesn't seem to be helping me. Maybe He's trying to tell me that I'm wasting my time. For the first time on his trip, home started to appeal to Abe . . .

Oregon and its Indian war, on the other hand, seemed like a foolish dream, one from which he was quite ready to wake up. He really didn't have any idea what he was heading into. He felt like he had been traveling forever. How much farther did this enormous country extend? How much longer would it take to reach Mary? What nonsense . . . she might not want any help from him even if he did make it through, he thought. He figured the date . . . December 13, nearly two weeks after the start of the war. What was the use?

Before noon, Abe took another walk down the ravine to inspect the flat. The storm might have slackened. He couldn't be sure. But there was no way to get across.

He went back to the spring. "If we can't make it tomorrow," Abe said, talking to the horse, "we'll head back. We'll just take it as a sign that's what we're supposed to do." Then he laughed nervously. He was talking to his horse . . . actually talking to the beast like it could understand him. What was this wilderness doing to him?

But the next morning broke crystal clear and calm. It was one of those days when the blue of the sky is so deep it looked unfamiliar, unreal. But it was cold, bitterly cold, even without a breeze. An inch of ice had formed on the spring during the night.

Abe built a large fire, then broke the ice for coffee water. Even with the exercise, the fire, and the coffee, he still wasn't warm by the time he mounted the horse.

At the bottom of the ravine, he faced a sight that was both spectacular and daunting. From the west to the north, the ground looked like a huge, frozen sea, absolutely flat and smooth. There wasn't a bush, a blade of grass, or tree anywhere to offer relief. The more Abe studied the edge of the flat, the more certain he was that this was the dried bed of a huge inland sea. With the snow sparkling in the sun, the sight was blinding. He couldn't imagine how anyone would have had the daring to cross that distance in the heat of summer. As he gazed, he even wondered about the wisdom of doing it in winter.

However, on the far horizon, almost directly northwest across the flats, rose some desert mountains that in ancient times must have extended as a headland into the water. At one end loomed a great, black butte—without question Black Rock. "Head directly toward it," Potter had told him.

Abe started with grit and made good time for the first hour. Then he realized that his horse was laboring excessively hard. He dismounted; underneath the dusting of snow, the surface was a thin crust over a soft, silty sand. Each step he took sank in and gave way as he tried to stride forward. The harder Abe tried, the less efficient his effort was until he was panting clouds of white breath that froze solid on his beard.

He stopped and watered his horse in his hat, then took a slug from the canteen himself. He had put heated water in the canteen, but it was already starting to freeze to the sides. Soon, he would have nothing to drink. He'd come a long way, but when he looked back, it was nothing compared to the distance that separated him from Black Rock. A chill settled in that he couldn't shake as he remounted.

Abe's eyes were hurting from the glare of the afternoon sun when he saw something moving out on the flat ahead of him. He blinked, and it went away leaving only the endless whiteness. But in a few minutes he saw it again, loping along at an angle across his path. He stared hard, his eyes aching against the glare. Finally he realized what it was: a lone wolf, heading who-knew-where?

He tied a bandanna across his face high up near his eyes. Then he pulled his hat low, leaving only a narrow slit to see through. It eased his eyes some until he was facing more directly into the afternoon sun. Then the brilliance was unbearable. His eyes felt like they were rolling in two bowls of liquid fire. He closed them for long stretches, and then braved only the narrowest squint. In time, his horse started to weave, and Abe had to continually neck rein him to keep him on course. Without the benefit of the hat or scarf, the horse had gone snowblind. When Abe realized what the problem was, he stopped, dug out his extra shirt and tied it across the horse's eyes.

But the horse refused to be ridden when it couldn't see at all. Finally Abe got off and led it.

A couple hours later, as he finally approached Black Rock, he saw clouds of smoke rising from its base. Somebody had a fire going, and from the looks of it, it was quite a fire. Abe's spirits lifted; there was someone else out there! Maybe it was a miner; Potter had said that prospectors were about the only people to go across the desert these days.

"Years ago," the liveryman had said, "when an emigrant was goin' across there, he was bein' harassed by Paiutes. Lacking lead, he picked up some heavy stuff and melted it in his campfire to make bullets. As it turned out, they were silver bullets, made from pure nuggets. Many a prospector's been looking for that lode ever since."

But the memory of Potter's tale reminded Abe of the possibility of Indians. If there was anyone out in this wilderness, it was most likely Indians. He slowed his pace. By now they had probably seen him. He desperately needed the water at the spring near the base of the butte, but he didn't like to take chances.

Abe thought it was funny how white the smoke was and how quickly it dissipated. Near the ground there were huge clouds, but they didn't float high or drift very far away. Something didn't look right. After a while, Abe realized why. It was not smoke at all but steam. There must be hot springs there.

He arrived at Black Rock as the sun was about to set. There was a slight sulfur smell in the air, but around the spring there was a small meadow. It was the stiff grass that had become familiar to him in this desert, but it was green, and the heat and steam of the springs had kept the snow off an acre or so. At its hottest, the springs were almost boiling as they bubbled up, but on down the line there were pools of pleasant warmth, and then ones cool enough to water his horse.

The roan seemed grateful to have the blindfold removed, and after a long drink, took to munching the grass.

This was an oasis if there ever was one! Abe thought. He dropped onto his back to relax. Then he realized that the nearer to the hot springs he moved, the warmer the ground became. He had a night of real comfort to look forward to, and he figured he deserved it after the ordeal of the last two days.

In fact, he thought, I ought to take a bath. He got up and tested the water in the pools until he found one large enough to swim in that was just bath temperature. He threw off his buffalo coat, stripped off his clothes, and jumped in. He lost himself in a cloud of steam that hung over the pool.

The hot spring was a luxury, warming his chilled bones and soaking the ache out of his muscles. He almost fell asleep right there, but he knew he'd have to scare up some wood for a fire before it got completely dark. Abe figured it was the first time in two days that he had been really warm.

Suddenly, the winter silence was broken by a wild whoop and the thunder of galloping hooves. Abe was so startled, he swallowed a mouthful of sulfur water, but the steam was too thick to see what was happening. As he scrambled for the edge of the pool and crawled out of the cloud of steam, he saw three Indians riding off into the purple gloom, his own horse in tow. Flapping on its back were his saddlebags with all his provisions, his blanket, and his rifle.

Chapter 11

*A*be's first impulse was to yell and run after the Indians. But as soon as he got to the edge of the snow, he slowed to a stop. It was no use. He was as naked as a peeled apple, and the temperature was still below zero. The relaxing heat of the hot springs wore off quickly, and the water on his body would soon freeze.

He walked back to the springs slowly. Without a horse, rifle, canteen, and food, Abe was in serious trouble, and he knew it. It was the shock of the situation as much as the cold that caused him to shiver and jerk uncontrollably.

It would be stupid to try to chase after the Indians. They could travel miles before the morning light would be bright enough to follow their trail. He'd heard that a man on foot could run down a horse if given enough time . . . but whoever said that probably hadn't figured on this kind of terrain or sub-zero weather.

Abe stood beside the steaming pool, his teeth chattering, hugging himself, and looking down at his pile of clothes. At least he had his pants, shirt, and coat and the buffalo robe. But at that moment he had to get warm enough to think straight.

He stepped down into the pool. The water seemed hot enough to burn his skin . . . but this was the same pool he'd been in a few minutes before. Soon, his body adjusted to the temperature . . . but he stayed near the edge where he could watch his clothes. He wasn't going to take a chance on the Indians coming back and stealing them, too.

I should have stripped my horse, Abe thought, still shivering.

If I'd only stripped my horse, I wouldn't be in such a fix. All my life I've always taken care of my horse before seeing to my own comfort. The one time I don't . . . look what happens.

Abe's mind sorted through all the other things he might have done to avoid this crisis—scout the area first to see if there were signs of anyone else . . . picket his horse closer by . . . not get into the pool where he couldn't see through the steam. The best plan, he thought, would have been not to come on this fool trip in the first place. I just might die out here yet.

He tried to calm himself and consider his options. He'd gotten across the Black Rock Desert, but a hundred miles of wilderness still lay ahead of him. If he could make better than thirty miles a day, he thought, that would be three days. Could he travel that hard without food? Could he make it between water holes without a canteen?

The initial shock of his loss was gone, but a deeper dread set in. Abe remembered the times after the tornado when he longed for the tragedy to be a nightmare from which he could awaken. If only he didn't have to face it, he'd thought. But he did, and he had survived.

He'd do the same again.

Abe got out of the water, dried himself as well as he could with his shirt and got dressed. Should he build a fire? The Indians would pinpoint his position if he did. On the other hand, they knew he was here and helpless. If they wanted anything more, they'd be back and take it as they pleased.

He built the fire and prayed that they wouldn't come back. When a small blaze was going among some tangled limbs of old sagebrush, Abe sat down. He checked his pockets, but there wasn't a scrap of jerky or a crumb of biscuit left in them.

He remembered something his father had often told him: "Abe, whatever you do, know your feelings . . . then rule them. The man who's angry but won't admit it, will be destroyed by his anger. The man who admits it, but doesn't control it, will also be destroyed."

Abe considered the idea. He wasn't angry. He was scared, but the advice probably still held. "O God," he prayed, "I really am scared. I don't know whether I've been wrong in coming out here, and I don't know how to figure it out. All I know is that I'm here, and there's a good chance I'm gonna die. Please help me use the good sense you gave me to do my best."

His father was right: admitting his fear helped. There was no bright light or voice booming from the burning bush in front of him, but somehow, he did believe that God had heard him. What makes a prayer real? he wondered. Maybe it's just honesty. He'd have to think about that sometime. "For now, thank you, God, for being there."

He felt like he was going to die, but the facts of the moment were that he was alive and warm and dry. He would fight the feeling with the facts. He might be hungry, but a person could go a long time without food—that was another fact he'd concentrate on as he fell asleep.

The next day was as cold and clear as the day before. Abe came instantly alert, remembering his plight. He drank hot water from the spring for his breakfast. It wasn't coffee, but it did warm him some.

In the day's light, he found the tracks of the Indians. They had followed him to the hot springs . . . not been waiting there for him as he'd supposed. He looked at the tracks coming as straight as an arrow across the flat of the Black Rock Desert. "What a fool I was to pay no attention to my back trail!" he chided himself. "I'll never let that happen again."

But the tracks of the departing Indians worried Abe even more. They continued along the Applegate Trail. The Indians had a long head start on him, but what if he caught up to them? On one hand, he might have a chance to retrieve his horse. But more than likely, they would see him coming and wait in ambush. This was their home, and he knew none of its secrets.

He started with caution. The land was no longer flat, and

over any little ridge, or in the next gully, they might be waiting. His caution slowed his travel. He wouldn't make thirty miles a day at this rate. He stepped up his pace in spite of the danger.

From time to time he could see rutted wagon tracks where the snow had blown away. It was a comfort to know he was on the trail and to imagine the hundreds of people who had passed this way in the past—men, women, families. People with hopes and dreams of a new life. People who overcame dangers and fears. That's what it took to live out here, and that's what he'd have to do if he was going to make it. His lack of food since noon the day before was starting to tell on his strength, but he remained determined.

Again Abe had to pull his hat low and tie his bandanna high over his face to protect his eyes from the ceaseless glare. The bandanna restricted his vision considerably, which was something he didn't like . . . knowing Indians were out there. But it would be worse if he went blind. He trudged on.

From time to time he grabbed a handful of snow and put it in his mouth for water, but the amount it chilled him as it melted made it less than worthwhile. After noon he stopped in a ravine. The wind had come up, and even with his hard pace, he was not keeping warm. He figured it was because of his lack of food for energy.

Abe found a rock with a basin hollowed out by ancient rains. Near it, he risked building a small fire. Then, in the basin he packed snow and put hot rocks from the fire on it. It melted, and soon he had water to drink without freezing his mouth. He put other heated rocks in his pockets, under his armpits, and held them in his hands. Finally he began to get warm again.

But he'd wasted over an hour before he got going again.

The frigid wind continued to blow until the shadows lengthened and the landscape turned an icy blue. From time to time the sagebrush was augmented by a lone juniper or two. The ridges took on the sharper look of an exposed lava flow. He was coming into a different country.

Abe walked on until it was almost dark. He had no idea how far he'd gone. Had he made his quota? His frequent falls had hindered his progress during the past hour. He knew he was staggering. Would he travel as far the next day? He decided he should get an earlier start.

Camp was a crack in the earth on the bank of a dry wash. He tried to build a fire, but couldn't keep it going, so he wedged himself back into the small crevice.

He was so tired . . . so very tired. Sleep was caving in on him. He worried that in this cold he might not wake up. But he couldn't help himself . . . he couldn't stay awake.

Abe awoke in the night and realized that his hands and feet were numb. It's frostbite . . . I'm freezing, he thought. I gotta get movin'. But when he tried to stand up, he fell over. There wasn't enough feeling in his feet to control his balance. His hands were like clubs on the ends of his arms. But they could move. Even in the dark he could see them close and open if he held them close to his face.

He crawled around, half on his hands and knees and half on his belly, trying to gather wood for a fire. Suddenly, something took off through the brush. It was big, and made no effort at silence. Was it an Indian? Had they come back to kill him?

Abe almost wished they had come back, just to have some contact with humans. Maybe they wouldn't kill him . . . maybe they'd take him to their camp and keep him as a slave. At least then he'd be warm and fed, and maybe someday he could escape. But he'd never heard of Indians taking men for slaves. Women, yes . . . and sometimes children that they could raise. But he'd only heard of men being scalped.

He gathered his little pile of sticks, then slapped his hands around him until some feeling came back, but they were still so stiff and clumsy that he wasted three of his precious matches before he got one to light.

When he went for more wood, there was again movement

in the brush, and he thought he saw a pair of eyes reflecting the dim light of his fire. Then they disappeared.

The next day was nearly the same as the one before, only he tired much quicker. In the night when his feet had been numb, he had apparently sprained his right ankle. This morning it was stiff and swollen and shot terrible pain up his leg as he tried to walk.

Abe had been on the trail for nearly an hour when he realized the Indian tracks no longer proceeded him. He wished he had noticed when they had stopped. They must have gone all the way to his camp the night before, but then he had been too tired to notice. He should have investigated around in the brush where he had heard movement. Were they stalking him? He couldn't understand it. Why didn't they make their move if they were after him? They were like phantoms . . . always out there, but never showing themselves.

As the day wore on, he had to stop often, trembling and faint with hunger. Once he blacked out and fell face down in the snow. He must have been there for quite some time. When he awoke, a hollow the size of a soup bowl had melted away from his nose. He got up and trudged on more slowly.

There were more juniper trees now and sometimes a cedar or scraggly pine. The wind had swept much of the snow from the trail, and the sagebrush was no longer covered. It made it easier on his eyes for there was something other than total white wherever he looked.

Twice in the afternoon he thought he saw movement out of the corner of his eyes, but when he turned, there was nothing there. He watched more carefully.

He found an old cedar pole, silver as a man's gray hair, and about six feet long. With a rock, he broke the stubs of branches off until it was smooth enough to carry. "It'll be my walking stick," he said aloud. "A fellow needs one of those." But his mind started playing with the idea of how he could use it to protect himself if the Indians attacked. It made very little difference to him that he was so weak that he could barely stand up. There was still some comfort in the idea of being able to defend himself.

The next morning, Abe was so stiff and cold that it took him a good twenty minutes to stand up. His body just wouldn't work. He stumbled and fell again and again before he had any rhythm to putting one foot before the other.

Again he saw movement . . . there, in the shadows under a line of trees. He was sure of it this time. In fact, he could barely make out three dark shapes . . . but Abe couldn't tell who—or what—they were. He crouched down to hide his own form behind the sagebrush. He clutched his walking stick. It was stout and strong, heavier than he needed for just walking.

It would be his defense if he were attacked. There's nothing else I can do, he reasoned. He remembered hearing about the Hutterites, those peace-church cousins of the Mennonites. When they first fled Nikolsburg, Austria, in 1528, they'd been known as the *stabler* (staff-bearers) in contrast to the general townspeople who were called *schwertler* (sword-bearers).

I have no intention of killing anybody, thought Abe. I'll just be a "stabler." I'll let my staff suffice . . . maybe it will save me. His mind worked on the problem. Maybe a peace-loving person could use some force if he didn't prepare to kill his enemy. The man who carried a sword was prepared to kill, but the man with only a staff . . . well, he might hurt someone, but he hadn't prepared to kill anyone.

The shadows had disappeared. Abe struggled to his feet and walked on for miles without remembering an inch of the path. Finally he looked around him and discovered he was completely off the trail. He couldn't even see it.

With great effort, Abe thought through what he had to do. He had to turn around and backtrack until he came again to the wagon tracks. But he'd worked so hard to come this far . . . and he was getting desperate to get through the wilderness. He knew he couldn't last much longer. To give up any of his hard earned ground seemed too much to ask. But he had to do it.

The patchy snow with his occasional footprints was his only guide. With all of his concentration, he watched the ground ahead, from one snow patch to the next. There were his prints . . . he must follow them, back . . . back . . . back . . .

At some point he realized there were wagon tracks on either side of his footprints. That's right, he thought foggily. I need to follow the wagon trail . . . the Applegate Trail . . . I need to stay right on it, put more footprints on the Applegate Trail and get to Oregon . . . Follow those who have gone before . . . One, two . . . One, two . . . Step on the old footprints . . . retrace the steps . . . one step, then another step. Somewhere in the back of his mind, the footprints looked strange in the snow. They were backwards. But Abe just kept following them. There was no other way.

Then he fell.

The shock startled him out of his daze. He looked around. He'd been going the wrong way! He'd been so intent on following his tracks to get back to the trail that he had continued to follow them even after he'd found it. He was losing control. He couldn't let that happen.

The afternoon shadows were getting longer, but he knew he had to stop and rest. He couldn't go on in this condition. Abe gathered some wood and carefully took one of his four remaining matches to light a fire. It struck, but his hand was shaking so badly that he hit it into a piece of snow as he attempted to hold it under the tinder. He risked one more match and succeeded.

Half an hour later, he felt better, picked up the trail going the right direction, and trudged on.

But his pursuers were still out there. Abe could feel it in his bones, and he watched more carefully. Then he saw something off to his left . . . not far away, no more than sixty yards.

It was a savage, all right, slinking along in a wolf skin. Abe had seen pictures of Indians hunting like that. How foolish to stalk him that way . . . he wasn't a dumb buffalo whom they could trick with their wolf costumes.

Then he saw two others to his right, closing in a little. All of them were dressed in those mangy wolf skins, down on all fours. They must be trying to spook him. Well, he'd show them . . . he'd make them get up and reveal themselves. He might be weak with cold and hunger, but he could still run faster than they could crawl.

He took off in a stumbling trot, looking back over both shoulders at the Indians. He was doing it . . . he didn't make them stand up, but he was leaving them behind. They couldn't keep up with him without giving away their cover. "I 'spect they've got bloody knees by now," Abe said to the icy wind, and he staggered on. He was starting to sweat.

An hour later, the sun was beginning to set. Abe was very cold and breathing in gasps. The sweating he'd been doing was making him colder. He couldn't understand it—shivering but still sweating.

And then he saw them again . . . straight behind him this time, making no pretense to hide . . . why did they keep hounding him? "On your feet, you savages!" Abe yelled, shaking his walking stick. One swerved to the side and ducked behind sagebrush, but the other two keep coming as though they hadn't even heard him.

Abe turned and started to run, and then fell. As he was scrambling to his feet, he looked back and couldn't believe his eyes. Those Indians were actually running toward him on all fours . . . why didn't they stand up?

He regained his feet and started to run. Something wasn't right . . . maybe he was imagining all this; maybe it was all in his head . . . maybe the snow glare had damaged his eyes, and he couldn't see right. He looked back, half expecting his pursuers to have disappeared. But they were still there . . . not running any longer—just coming on with their lanky crawl, noses to the ground.

Abe couldn't run anymore. He was falling every fifty feet. He had to walk. He leaned hard on his staff. He was sweating heavily, but colder than ever. He tried to say something outloud, to shake off the silence broken only by the whine of the wind . . . and realized that his speech was so slurred that he couldn't understand himself.

He looked back. The Indians were gone . . . maybe it had all been a dream after all. Now he was shivering in great uncontrollable jerks, his breath shallow and irregular. Three days of hard travel without food was taking its toll; his body no longer had the energy to hold off the cold. The wind was winning; he was losing.

Abe knew his body temperature was dropping. Without the help of outside heat, there would be no recovery. He'd gone below the point of spontaneous return.

He collapsed under a dead juniper tree and with clumsy effort, managed to break some limbs to the ground. Then he pulled some dry sagebrush over. When he had prepared his pile, he got out his last two matches. With shaking hands, Abe wedged one match into a crack in the tree to keep it safe. Then he found a stone to strike the other on. He steadied it between his knees and drew the match across it.

A spark, but no flame.

He tried again. No luck. And then on the third try, a brilliant flame burst into the dark twilight. But no sooner had it flared, than a gust of wind blew it out.

Desperation bordering on panic settled into the pit of his stomach. Moving his body to shield his work from the wind, Abe carefully retrieved the last match. He rallied all his strength to his shaking hands and prepared to strike the match . . . when a movement from the gloom caught his eye.

It was those sly savages again, out there in the brush, just beyond where he could see them clearly. Well, Abe no longer cared. He had to get warm or he would die anyway. He turned back and struck the match. It flared the first time, then withered down to a feeble glow. He held it carefully, frightened that his shaking hand would put it out. "O God, let it burn . . . let it burn."

Finally the little flame grew, and Abe held it under the tinder. The tinder caught, and flames licked upward. Abe added more wood until the fire was roaring, but he still wasn't getting any warmer. He broke off some dried grease wood from nearby brush and threw it on the fire.

Abe sat close to the blaze as it roared higher. The fire was stinging his skin, but he was still getting colder. He was losing, and he knew it.

He looked out to the edge of the firelight to see if the Indians were there laughing at him. His vision was blurred, but the shadows were there. Two were sitting on their haunches staring at him. A third paced back and forth on all fours just at the edge of the firelight. Their eyes glowed with a cold fire.

They really did look like wolves, thought Abe vaguely.

The fire leaped higher and caught in the limbs of the dead juniper tree as Abe passed out.

Chapter 12

*T*he snarling tornado roared at Abraham Miller as he clung to the reins of his flimsy buckboard. He was racing recklessly into the storm's snapping jaws, its teeth ready to snag him on its next round. And then it had him, twisting, dragging him face down across the gravel drive, trying to rip him apart. The breaking apple trees along the lane cracked and popped like rifles near his ears. And then it flung him up into the air, higher and higher until there was pure and blessed silence. He was floating in the frigid ether. He was dying.

He looked down on the patchwork of the Indiana farm land, fields and woods cut by streams and roads. He knew that place. It was his lane, going to his house. Everything was so small. The storm was gone, its gray clouds nothing but a memory on the far horizon. The memory was bitter. He hated it for what it had done to him.

And what it had done was plain enough to see when Abe looked down. The farm was a shambles, nothing but kindling where the house had stood. He knew the bodies of his family were there, not one left alive. At least now, he and they were together in death. No longer separated.

Then Miller noticed somebody walking around in the pasture. It was a man trying to catch the team from his buckboard. The horses were still connected by a harness, though it was half-torn apart. They were terrified and wouldn't come to the man. But the man knew horses, and he finally caught them.

And then as Miller looked closer, he realized that the man was himself, Abe. As tiny as he appeared down there in that field, there was no question. It was him.

Miller watched as Abe returned to the rubble of the house, calming the shy team all the way. Then he hitched the remains of the harness to a big rope that had been tied around a beam of the house. Abe slowly eased the horses forward until they withdrew the beam. Then he went back for another, and another. Sometimes he stopped and pulled boards out by hand.

Miller realized that his vantage point was closer. He could see more clearly, as though he was only about treetop high. As he watched himself, he knew what was going to happen next, and he tried to call out a warning for Abe not to proceed, but no sound came from his frozen lungs. There below, Abe reached into the rubble to pull out the body of his father, broken and limp as a bag of loose laundry. He carried him out into the yard and laid him there in the sun, but there was no life in the man.

Back Abe went, and in time found his mother, sisters, and brothers—all but three-year-old Toby. Toby didn't seem to be there. He searched for more than an hour and was taking courage, hoping that the child hadn't been home when the twister struck.

But Miller knew different. He knew where Toby was. Toby's crushed, bloody body was in the corner under the toppled canning shelves. It would be better if Abe didn't find him, thought Miller. I should get him away from there. It's only minutes now, until he realizes that all the red in the corner isn't just broken tomato jars. I must warn him. But there was no way, no way at all to make contact.

Miller watched in agony as Abe went over to the pile and began to move the boards and broken jars aside. And then Abe let out a long hollow howl, as though he were lost in an endless tunnel, and pulled the sad body of his baby brother from the garbage. He held him close and sat on an upturned wooden bucket. There Abe rocked back and forth, moaning in a quiet, helpless way until sundown when Elder Daniel Brenneman rode up on his horse.

Miller couldn't watch anymore and turned away to the darkening sky.

How long he looked into that blackness, he had no way of knowing. But finally somebody roused him with a gentle shake . . .

"Come on, buddy. Let's wake up."

Abe came to in a fog. The air was cold, and he was in a small tent, dimly lit by a cyclone lantern. A man in an army uniform was stooping beside him. Vivid in Abe's mind was the experience of watching himself find his family after the tornado. The memory was so fresh that he felt like he was somewhere near home, maybe at Brenneman's or somewhere. But an army sergeant? Nothing was familiar.

"Who . . . are you?" Abe asked.

"Sergeant Curtis Brown, First Cavalry. Who are you?"

"Name's Abe Miller."

"What're you doin' out here in this wilderness, Miller?"

It all came back to Abe with a rush. "I . . . I'm on my way to Oregon . . . to Lost River. Where am I now?"

"You're at Camp Bidwell, and mighty lucky to be here, too."

Abe thought about that, and remembered the shadows, stalking . . . stalking. "Did you . . . did you kill the Indians?"

"Indians? Didn't see no Injuns. Almost didn't see you if it weren't for that fire you lit. You came mighty close to dyin' of exposure, though. It took us forever to get you warmed up. Last night and all today we didn't know whether you'd ever come 'round or not."

Abe struggled to sit up, but was too exhausted. As the sergeant asked question after question, eventually the story came out about his trek across the Black Rock Desert, about the Indians stealing his horse and then following him for two days, torturing and teasing him in their crazy wolf skins.

The sergeant snorted. "Well, I have no doubt you lost your

horse and gear to some thieving Paiutes. They're always raid-
ing anyone they can find out there. But they wouldn't foller a
man for two days. Just ain't like 'em . . . with no reason, that is.
Besides, the only tracks we saw where you built that fire were
from the wolves we ran off when we came up."

"Wolves . . ."

"You better believe it. Here, take a look at this boot of yours.
They dragged you twenty feet across the snow and ice to get
you away from that fire. If we hadn't come along when we did
and fired a few shots, they'd a been fightin' over you for supper."

Abe looked at the boot the man held up in the dim light.
There were several deep tooth marks. One fang had gone all
the way through in the back, right above the heel. As reality
sank in, Abe felt both frightened and foolish.

"We was out on patrol," the sergeant continued, "a bit farther than we usually go this time of year, when one of my men
noticed a tree burning, way across the valley . . . a good six or
seven miles.

"Well, I got out my glass but couldn't figure it out. That tree
was burning for no good reason. There hadn't been any storm
or lightning for a couple days, and no self-respectin' Injun
would blaze a tree if all he needed was a cookin' fire. With my
glass, I couldn't see no wagon, no horses, or anything else. We
come mighty close to ridin' on, but my curiosity got the best of
me, and we headed on over. And there you were . . . two inches this side o' death itself."

Abe did his best to thank the sergeant for saving his life
before drifting back into an exhausted sleep.

It took him another day to recover enough to leave the tent.
During that time, he often pondered his vision of the tornado.
He could finally remember finding each of his family members
in the wreckage of the house, and that was a great relief
though the memory wasn't pleasant. But now there was a new
mystery. What had happened to him when he was uncon-

scious? It seemed so much more than a regular dream, both in its vividness and in the elements of reality—the cold, the memory of being dragged across something rough, the sense of dying. He realized he might never know the answers, but it nagged at him.

Once he could leave the tent, Abe began trying to arrange to get to Linkville. He was now so late that Davis would probably have already come and gone. But by now the war would really be heating up . . . he didn't dare delay. Camp Bidwell's primary purpose was to monitor any Indian movements in the region—especially given the Modoc troubles to the west. But because of its small size, it had no extra horses, not even one to loan Abe for a trip to Linkville.

"However, Miller," said Sergeant Brown, "we're as short of men as we are of ridin' stock around here. Can you handle a team?"

"I can handle a team of six . . . pulling anything," said Abe with confidence.

"Well, these will be mules, but there'll only be four of 'em. You got yourself a ride at least halfway to Linkville, if you'll teamster a supply wagon we're sending over to Tule Lake tomorrow. And you shouldn't have any trouble getting from there on up to Linkville."

"What kind of supply wagon?"

"Mostly firewood, believe it or not. There ain't much of it over near them lava beds. There'll also be some commissary stores and much needed ammunition. Captain Bernard's G Troop is camped over there near Louis Land's ranch. He thinks them Modocs are gonna keep him in the field longer than he planned, and he's desperate for the supplies."

"I don't think I want to be hauling ammunition," Abe said cautiously. He didn't want to be helping the army in the war effort.

"Don't you worry," the sergeant laughed. "We're not about to take any chance on those savages getting their hands on this stuff. You'll have an escort of six cavalrymen plus another man ridin' shotgun beside ya. All we want is someone who can drive."

"Well, that wasn't exactly my concern," Abe muttered. But he was reluctant to speak of his pacifist convictions to a military man. And besides, he argued with himself, he did have to get on with his trip. It was a question of the lesser of two evils. If he drove the wagon, he was helping the army. But if he didn't go with the wagon, his whole goal of stopping the war would be further delayed.

"All right," he agreed. "Show me those mules."

Chapter 13

*A*t dawn on December 20, Abe and his escorts rolled out of camp. It was going to be a hard haul of more than seventy miles down around the bottom of Goose Lake and then over to Tule Lake. The soldier riding shotgun was not at all pleased with having a greenhorn civilian along—especially one who had so recently been sick in bed. He assumed Abe wouldn't be able to last out the trip and he'd have to take over . . . maybe at a critical moment.

At first Abe's wagon companion did not talk much, but finally he warmed up. Private Fritz Kresgy was his name, about the same age as Abe. He'd been a hardluck gold miner before he joined the army. "Yeah . . . got a wife and three kids I plan to bring up from Shasta as soon as the weather gets better," the young man drawled. Unfortunately, Kresgy hadn't been in the army long enough to give Abe any information about the history of the war, and he'd never heard of Reno or Mary Bauder. As far as the Modocs were concerned, Kresgy had only heard that they'd retreated to caves in the lava beds and were holding out there.

The sun was at high noon the next day when they sighted Captain Bernard's headquarters on a bay forming the southeast corner of Tule Lake. The landscape was not what Abe expected when he thought of a lake. Tules—tall, coarse reeds—grew high around the shores of the shallow lake, but the surrounding country was still very rough and desert-like. With only a couple miles to go, the escort began to relax. It looked like there would be no trouble.

And then a shot from a high bank near the road just missed Abe and slammed into the offside wheel mule. Abe could see in an instant that the wound was a serious lung shot, but he whipped the team into a mad run anyway.

"Get down there on that tongue and cut that mule loose!" he yelled at Kresgy.

"You gotta be crazy!" Kresgy yelled back above the rattle of the wagon and the heavy fire coming from all around them. "That'd be suicide!"

"That mule's ready to collapse," yelled Abe, noticing the bright red blood pumping from its side. "If we don't cut it loose, this whole wagon's gonna crash . . . an' if that don't get us, the Indians will. Now *that's* suicide—so get to it!" But when Kresgy didn't move, Abe thrust the reins into his hands and climbed down himself.

The road was rough, and the whole rig heaved and bucked. Twice Abe nearly slipped off the tongue before he cut the mule free . . . not a moment too soon, either. The animal didn't even get out of the path of the wagon before it stumbled and fell, the wheels bouncing over its legs.

Abe glanced back at the mule as they raced on, but what he saw shocked him even more. The private who'd been riding escort closest to the wagon—a man named Smith—was lagging. He'd been shot right in the head. And then he fell, landing face first on the rocky road. As Abe watched, another escort, Private Donahue, stiffened and fell forward in the saddle, barely hanging on. Bullets were firing from everywhere, and a band of Indians were closing in hard on horseback.

Just then a rescue party from the army camp came riding hard past the flying wagon and drove off the attackers. In a swirl of flying snow, Abe brought the lathered mules to a halt in Bernard's camp.

Without Captain Bernard's quick response in sending out a rescue party, the wagon, its supplies, and the men with it would have been lost. Later, Donahue died of his spinal wound, and when the rescue party brought in Smith's corpse, it had already been stripped and mutilated. Captain Bernard said it was the first time during these hostilities that the Modocs had scalped a victim.

Abe tried to quiet himself as he sipped a hot cup of coffee. His initiation to the Modoc Indian War was more than he'd bargained for. This bloody attack and the theft of his horse and gear in the Black Rock Desert had sapped his sympathy for Indians. Frankly, he was ready to be through with them. But as the hot coffee warmed his insides, well-taught theories about war and peace from his upbringing admonished him: if he hadn't been driving a military supply wagon—one carrying ammunition at that—he wouldn't have been attacked. It was his involvement with the war effort that had caused him to be a target of its violence.

But this time the answer seemed too simple. He'd been minding his own business, utterly innocent, when the Paiutes stole his horse at the hot springs. No, the neat answers didn't always work.

The next day was cold and brisk. Large white clouds tumbled across the blue sky. The sun, when it shone at all, offered little warmth. Abe borrowed a horse and rode on to Linkville with Private Kresgy who had been assigned to continue beyond the supply run as the weekly courier between Camp Bidwell and Fort Klamath.

"I've got to get on up to Fort Klamath before nightfall," Kresgy said. "But I'll stop in Linkville and get a bite to eat with you. George Nurse's hotel's not bad . . . we can get a good meal there. I haven't found a better place to eat since I last saw my wife."

Abe felt strange keeping company with a U.S. military man, but he was beginning to like the young soldier who always mentioned his family.

Linkville was a bustling town on the southern tip of Klamath Lake. It was crowded with war correspondents, military personnel, and families of settlers who had temporarily moved into town to escape the hostilities.

Abe followed Kresgy into the hotel only to discover there were no vacant rooms. "Well, come on, Miller. We need something to eat anyway. You can find some place to stay later."

When they entered the hotel saloon, three men were standing at the bar and twice that many sitting at tables eating a meal prepared in the kitchen out the side door.

One of the men at a table jumped up so fast when he saw Abe that his chair tipped over backwards. "I thought you'd never get here!" Jonathan Davis grinned under his big mustache. "I was fixin' to leave two days ago until I overheard some army guy tell how they found a man near dead out in the wilderness. He didn't know the name or nothin', but the description sounded enough like you, that I thought I'd wait a little longer. But you were coming up by train . . . it wasn't you, was it?"

"I'm afraid it was," Abe admitted. He and Kresgy sat down with Davis and ordered two bowls of hearty stew and biscuits. Between mouthfuls, Abe told Davis about his attempted shortcut.

After they ate, Davis insisted that Abe use his bed in the hotel to get some rest. After saying good-bye to Kresgy, Abe followed Davis on up to his room. He wondered if Davis had learned about the war and Mary's safety, but he fell asleep before he even had a chance to ask.

Abe slept straight through until the next morning. He didn't know where Davis slept for the night—probably on the floor—but when Abe awoke, Davis was sitting near the window with a bowl of water and a piece of a mirror, shaving.

As soon as they went down for breakfast, Abe asked Davis to fill him in on anything he'd learned about the war.

"Well, I have no way of telling whether your theory about Meacham and Odeneal is right. I've only seen Meacham once. He's still a prominent man in this neck of the woods—into politics, I think. I hear he's one of Oregon's delegates to the Electoral College. He's supposed to be headin' back to Washington any day now. So there's not much chance of you talkin' to him.

"But there's one other thing I've discovered. This Bauder is a very powerful, ruthless man. If he caught wind of what you're up to, your life wouldn't be worth a plug nickel. In fact, I stuck around here for the one purpose of warnin' you: I think you ought to let the whole matter drop and get out of here."

"But what about Mary?" asked Abe.

"Mary Bauder? Aw, she's here in town."

Chapter 14

*I*t didn't take too many inquiries to find out that Mary Bauder was staying with the widow Morgan who owned a nice house on the south side of town. A gray fog enveloped the town, but Abe didn't have any trouble finding the house. He didn't know what he'd say or how Mary would respond; he just knew he had to see her.

"Abe Miller!" she said, her eyes widening with surprise when she answered the door. "What are you doing here? I thought you were in Kansas."

"Hi, Mary," Abe said, twirling his hat in his hands . . . and then he could think of nothing more to say. He had dreamed of her dozens of times, of rescuing her from her father or out of the middle of an Indian war. He'd imagined taking a quiet walk with her in a grassy meadow. He had remembered the little wisps of dark hair that broke away and curled gently on the pale skin of her regal neck. He'd even dreamed of more— enough to make him blush. But he'd never planned what he'd say when he met her again.

"I . . . I've already been to Kansas." He shrugged and grinned. He knew it was no explanation, but he couldn't think of anything else.

"Well, come in . . . It's much too cold to stand out on the porch on a morning like this. You look awfully thin . . . what's happened? Oh, excuse me . . . I want you to meet Mrs. Morgan."

Abe paid very little attention as Mary introduced him to the matronly widow. He hoped his feeble greetings sufficed as he tried to plan how he would explain himself to Mary. Soon Mary's hostess excused herself and went to the kitchen, and Abe and Mary sat facing each other in Mrs. Morgan's stiff parlor chairs.

Mary was as beautiful as Abe had remembered—even more so, if that was possible.

"Tell me, why are you in Linkville?" Mary asked again. "Surely the Mennonites aren't thinking of starting a colony in Oregon."

"No . . . actually, I didn't stay with the survey team. I came across something in the newspaper . . . about the war and all."

"About the war?"

Abe didn't know whether to tell her about his notion of stopping the war or about his concern for her safety. There in the widow's sitting room, decorated with its Christmas ribbons and tree, both reasons seemed foolish. Mary obviously wasn't in any danger. And the war? Well, it wasn't so clear anymore. Images of the Paiutes riding off with his horse and Smith's bloody face plowing into the rocky road flashed across Abe's mind.

"Davis is here with me, too," offered Abe lamely.

"Davis?"

"Yeah, you remember . . . Jonathan Davis, that little man on the train. The one with the big mustache and the bowler hat."

"Oh yes. He helped me ask around about my father when we didn't know where he was. I remember him. But . . . what's he doing here? You two weren't traveling together on the train, were you?"

"No, but we kinda hooked up later, and he agreed to come to Oregon with me. He always wanted to come out here anyway. He says he wants to live here someday."

Mary studied Abe's face. "But you still haven't told me why you came out here."

Abe took a big breath. Would it be Mary or the peace plan? "It was you," he admitted. "I read in the paper about the Indian war starting on Lost River, and . . . I knew that's where you lived. The news clipping even mentioned the Bauder ranch. Anyway, I was afraid your father was letting you walk right into the middle of all this trouble, so . . ." Abe shrugged.

"So, you . . . what?"

"I was afraid you might be in danger, so I . . . I . . . came out here to see if you were okay," Abe blurted.

"That's ridiculous!" Mary laughed. "That's no reason to come all the way across the country."

"Why not?" bristled Abe, feeling embarrassed but not wanting to show it. "Your father didn't seem to care all that much when you were on the train."

"Well . . . well, Papa doesn't think there's much danger," Mary said flatly. "In fact, I . . . I came to stay in town on my own. But now the danger's past."

"What do you mean? You're not going back out to the ranch, are you?"

"Why not? The army's crawling all over the country now, and the Modocs have retreated into the Lava Beds. They're far enough away that the ranch is safe. Besides, I can't stay here with Mrs. Morgan indefinitely."

"I don't think it's so safe out there," Abe snorted. "We were attacked yesterday riding in here, and two men were killed. The rest of us barely escaped."

"What do you mean? Where?" asked Mary.

"At the south end of Tule Lake, near someone's ranch . . . named Louis Land, I think."

"Oh, that's nearly fifteen miles from our place. I think it will be okay. But how come you were down at Tule Lake, anyway? That's not on the road from Yreka."

And so the story came out about Abe's effort to take a cross-country shortcut from Winnemuca. Mary smiled and shook her head during his story. He didn't know whether to be embarrassed for trying such a dangerous crossing in winter or proud that he had made it. But Mary seemed both amused and impressed.

"I think you're plain crazy to do such a wild thing, Abe Miller. And I don't for a minute believe your story that you came all this way just because you were worried about my safety. What was your real reason?"

How could she know there was something more? Abe wondered. Had he been that clumsy in saying he was worried about her safety, or was she just fishing? Still, he wasn't the kind of person who could deny his purpose when asked so directly.

"There was another reason," Abe began, looking down at his boots. "It all started when I read that newspaper story about the war. I remembered what you and your father were arguing about the night I first met you. You accused him of blackmail for getting Indian Superintendent Meacham replaced by Odeneal . . . and after readin' the paper, I put two and two together. If your father really used blackmail to get Meacham replaced, then he was actually responsible for starting a war—a war in which people were already dying, right when we were on the train."

Mary frowned. "That's a mighty big accusation, Abe Miller. Why does that make my father responsible for starting this war?"

Abe swallowed . . . but it was too late to back down. "Because Meacham was trying to work for peace, and that's why your father had him replaced. Odeneal is his puppet to press a military solution that could destroy the tribe forever. It was your father's way of saving his range land from being turned into a reservation."

Mary got up and walked over to a window. She was silent several minutes, then she said quietly, "I never thought of it like that . . . but what can anyone do about it now? Father would never admit that."

Abe's heart beat faster. She believed him! "Well, the first person I need to tell is Meacham. He probably suspects foul play anyway."

Mary turned to face Abe. "You'll not see him for a couple months. He left this morning for Washington."

"This morning?"

"As far as I know. We talked yesterday afternoon, and he was going to ride the mail wagon down to Yreka today. It usually leaves at sunrise."

"For Washington, you say? Maybe he's on to something and heading back there to get it straightened out."

"I doubt it. He's on the Electoral College, and he went back there to serve for the presidential election."

Abe frowned. Meacham was a key figure in his plan. He paced thoughtfully on the plush carpet. "If he just left this morning, do you think there's a chance I could catch him?"

"Well, the mail wagon probably left a couple hours ago, but I suppose you might. However, there's nothin' Meacham can do now, Abe. Why don't you let it be? It's out of your hands." A flicker of anxiety passed over Mary's face.

"No it's not," Abe protested. "I think there's a whole lot he could do, especially if he's going to Washington. He could flush out the bureaucrat who removed him as the Indian superintendent and confront him about yielding to your father's blackmail. That would be perfect. I've got to catch him. Is there a livery in town?" Abe said, putting on his hat.

"Oh, Abe, don't mix in this any further," pleaded Mary, laying a hand on his arm. "It's not your fight. I'm really glad to see you, and I wanted to believe that you only came back here to see me. But somehow I knew there was something more. It's a noble concern you have, but it's an impossible one. You'd easier stop a river flowin' than stop the course of history. And that's what you're trying to do."

Abe knew that both rivers and history had been stopped before, but he wasn't going to argue the point. He had to leave if he was going to catch Meacham. "I'm sorry, Mary. It's something I've got to do. I'll see you later . . . and I really did come here to see you," he said as he went out the door.

A half hour later, Abe was headed south after Meacham, riding hard on a long-legged bay through a cold, clinging mist. Things were going better. Soon he'd get to talk to Meacham, and he had already seen Mary. She had been glad to see him. More than that, she had cared whether he rode off after Meacham or not. He felt a strange excitement. Maybe there was hope for something more between them.

For the first fifteen miles Abe passed several signs of a military presence in the area. Heavy wagons had deeply rutted the road. At one place, through the fog, he could see the ugly scars of a winter camp beside the road. Later, two detachments of men passed him moving north. But where the road to Yreka cut off to the east, there were fewer signs of travel.

Abe pushed his horse as hard as he dared knowing that he might still have a long way to go before catching Meacham. What worried him most was the chance that Meacham would get to Yreka before he caught him. Abe didn't know when the stage would leave, but if it was a close connection, Meacham could be on it and gone by the time Abe got there. Trying to overtake a fast moving stage would be even harder than catching the old mail wagon.

He was going over the alternatives in his mind, not paying much attention to the road, when his horse shied as he came around a bend. Three horsemen were blocking his path . . . Indians. Abe pulled his horse to a hard stop just ten feet from them. They sat on their horses without moving or saying a word, but Abe noticed that all three had their rifles casually pointed in his direction.

Abe's horse was snorting and prancing, trying to catch its breath and not liking the smell of the Indians. Still the Indians did not move. In the swirling fog, Abe might have been tempted to think that they were gray stone statues except that one of their horses shifted its weight from its right to left foot and switched its tail.

Nearly a minute of silence passed, though it felt much

longer. Abe wondered what he should do. Should he turn back? Or should he try to pass through them?

"Morning," he said and nudged his horse forward. If they meant him harm, he'd have a hard time getting away, so he might as well try to get through.

They still said nothing, but the center one turned his horse sideways, completely blocking Abe's way.

"Mind if I pass?" Abe asked in as friendly a voice as possible.

"Wait," one said. And then out of the brush and crashing down a high bank from the right came a fourth Indian. His face was grotesquely scarred, twisted into a mocking grimace that made Abe shudder. He wore a flat-topped, brimless fur hat and had his white man's coat buttoned all the way to the top in a way that made him look like one of the first Mennonite immigrants to arrive from Russia.

"Where's your gun?" the Indian demanded.

Abe's mouth was dry. He tried to swallow. "I don't carry one."

The leader spoke something in Modoc to one of the other warriors who came quickly forward to pull back Abe's buffalo coat. There was more talk in Modoc as Abe was briefly searched.

"You follow us," the one with the scar ordered in firm but quiet words. Then he and the other Modocs turned and rode off through the brush, leaving Abe sitting in the road. The thought crossed Abe's mind that he could race on down the trail before they knew what he'd done, but there had been a strange confidence in the Indian's words that caused Abe to follow even though no one was holding a gun on him.

A few minutes of following the Indians through the wet brush, fighting it away from his face and ducking to avoid being swept off his horse, and Abe realized why the Indians had no concern for his escape. The narrow game trail they followed through the draw came up a rise to meet the main road again after the road had followed a more leisurely route around the rim of the hollow. The Indians' shortcut would have put them back on his trail long before he could have gotten past the intersection no matter how fast he might have ridden.

Chances are, thought Abe, they had some equal trick to cover me if I had headed back toward Linkville. He followed the Indians in silence. Abe had always considered himself pretty good at keeping his bearings, but the trail twisted and turned so often that in the drizzle, Abe soon lost any sense of where he was. The country was getting more rugged and rocky, strewn with huge boulders.

That's when Abe realized where the Indians were taking him: into the Lava Beds where Captain Jack and his band of Modocs were said to be holed up.

Chapter 15

The boulders became more and more frequent until Abe could see very little earth or foliage between them. The trail was so hard to follow that Abe could not pick it out twenty feet ahead or behind. But the Indians knew where to guide their horses so they had a flat, solid place to plant their hooves.

Then the boulder field ended as they met the mass of black lava that had once been a molten slug creeping across the earth. As it had cooled, deep fissures and cracks developed everywhere in its surface as though it were severely chapped skin. Some breaks were inches deep, some feet deep, and some Abe couldn't see to the bottom of. Here there was no visible trail at all, but somehow the Indians knew how to navigate through the devil's garden.

Abe could see that the edges of the lava were sharp and rough, and once when his horse lurched, Abe looked down to see a mean gash in its left rear pastern where it had brushed the edge of a volcanic knife. In some places the lava lost its dull rough surface and appeared shiny. At first Abe thought they were little springs seeping through the rocks, but then he realized that these ribbons in the lava were more like glass, some smoky in color, some streaked with a rusty red, and some as black as enamel. Where they broke at some fissure, the corners looked like razors.

When the horsemen finally stopped, they were in a deep crevasse as wide as a town street. It was easy for Abe to imagine that he had ridden down some street with solid buildings on each side made of black brick. Then he saw that the

Indians had the end roped off for their corral of horses.

Abe's captors dismounted and motioned for him to follow them as they walked into a large cave. The cave was a perfectly round tunnel of about fifteen feet diameter. The sides were smooth and almost looked polished. Abe had never seen anything like it. On the sandy floor of the tunnel, the Indians had set up camp. The amount of possessions and supplies demonstrated that they were prepared for a long and comparatively comfortable stay. When the children saw Abe, they stopped their play and followed as the four warriors led Abe through the family campsites.

The scout party stopped in front of an Indian seated beside a small fire. He was a sad-eyed man with a kind face and a square jaw. Abe guessed his age at thirty-five. Abe later learned his name was Kintpuash, the Modoc chief the whites called Captain Jack. Back in the shadows sat a sour youth with pouting lips and wide eyes.

"Who is this?" asked Captain Jack.

"I'm Abe Miller. I come in peace."

"So do all whites," snorted Jack. "That's why we live in a hole like the coyote." The scarfaced man then said something in Modoc. Jack laughed. "No, no. He's got a gun, and if you didn't find it, then he's all the more dangerous. Search him again, Scarfaced Charley, and then shoot him with it." Captain Jack turned back to the fire, uninterested.

Two of the braves who had met Abe on the road stepped forward and ripped off his coat.

"But I tell you," protested Abe as he was being roughly searched, "I come in peace. I belong to a people called Mennonites . . . we follow Jesus' teachings and do not think this fighting is good. I was going after Mr. Meacham to help him stop the war between you and the whites."

"No gun," the braves said as they ended their search.

"Then he dropped it on the way," growled the voice sitting in the shadows. "But I do not need a gun to kill him." Later Abe learned the sour-faced youth was called Hooker Jim.

Jack looked up again. "Why did you follow Meacham?"

"Because I have news that could make him the Indian superintendent again . . . and I think Meacham would work for peace. Don't you want this war ended?"

The Indians in the cave muttered angrily among themselves until Jack spoke. "We do not want war. All we want is to go back to our home on Lost River. We are willing to pay for any cattle we have killed. We don't want to fight anymore."

"Good," said Abe. "Then I'm sure this thing can be settled."

Jack laughed hollowly. "You are crazy. I call you Crazy Abe. Anyone who rides into Modoc country without a gun is crazy. And if you think you can stop the war, you are twice crazy."

"He is not crazy," growled Hooker Jim. "I see him before in his buffalo robe and flat hat. He drive army wagon. He is no peace man. You are old squaw, Kintpuash, to believe this liar . . ." Hooker Jim switched to Modoc and continued in harsh tones, obviously berating Captain Jack. The other warriors joined in with words of approval. Only Scarfaced Charley remained silent.

"He is a sly one," continued Hooker Jim again in English. "And you are the fools to lead him into our camp. Before now the army did not know our position. He should die."

"Enough," said Captain Jack. "We have plenty of time to kill him."

At that, Hooker Jim got up and walked away. Scarfaced Charley and the other warriors left as well, and Abe was left standing before Captain Jack. He tried to ask the young chief what was happening, but Jack ignored him as though he were not there. In fact, everyone in the whole camp ignored him. Even the youngest children refused to make eye contact with him.

Abe wandered around as though he were a ghost. He found his buffalo coat in a heap on the floor and gratefully put it on. The temperature in the cave was very cold. At one point Abe took a torch and ventured deep into the cave until he found a frozen river. On it lay quarters of beef, some fish, and baskets of seeds. Nowhere did he find fresh water.

When he got back to the camp, all the warriors were gone. The women and children and a couple old men were eating and laughing together. No one offered Abe any food.

The absence of guards gave Abe his chance to make an escape, and he worked his way toward the mouth of the cave. The gray fog still hung low, making a near ceiling to the "street" down which he had come. His horse was gone along with all the other horses, but there was no one to stop him, so he left.

He crept along getting bolder with every step until he came to where he and his escorts had entered the lava canyon. He turned up the narrow trail and started for home. The fog was a little thinner, but he could not see more than a quarter of a mile. He had only gone a short distance before he realized he was off the path by which he had entered the area. In fact, there was no more path, and he was having to climb over rocks and fissures, sharp ridges and ragged cracks. It was late in the afternoon, and he was sure he was headed north. It gave him hope until he looked at his boots. His good boots were cut like someone was making rawhide thongs of them. Much more of this sharp terrain and he'd be walking barefoot, and on a bloody pair of feet at that.

Abe looked back the way he had come. He'd been traveling an hour, but he doubted that he had covered more than a mile. In front of him loomed a deep crevice too wide to jump across. He tried to climb down, but its depth seemed to have no end, and the lava was so sharp that it had scratched his hands raw after only a few minutes' effort. He climbed back out, and looked both directions for a way around. Finally he struck out to the right, thinking the crack narrowed in that direction, but it was a ruse. It twisted and turned, but never became cross-able.

Abe turned back the other way. In this direction the crevice obviously got wider, but the sides became less steep. He continued until he found where he could climb down to the bottom. The bottom was only about a yard wide and like a creek bottom, but the other side remained insurmountable.

As the canyon got wider, Abe suddenly had the eerie feeling that he had been in it before. Again it was the wide city street with the "black brick buildings" on either side. He walked on, and then became more sure as he saw a pile of fresh horse manure. This was the very canyon of the Modocs' hideout. He had accomplished no more than to ruin his boots.

When he got back to the cave, all the warriors had returned, but the horses were not there. Apparently, they had been left elsewhere for food and water. When Abe entered the cave, the Indians continued to ignore him. No one offered him anything to eat or drink, and he was becoming desperately thirsty. There were about a hundred people in the camp, including the women and children, and Abe couldn't figure out how they were all able to keep from taking any notice of him without having to avert their eyes quickly. To have turned away from him would have at least acknowledged that he was there to be avoided, but there wasn't even that much recognition.

Abe was surprised that the camp had no dogs. It was getting to the point where he would have welcomed even a bark or snarl.

Finally Abe walked over to Captain Jack and bluntly asked for food and water, but the chief refused to respond.

That night, Abe curled up in his coat on the sandy floor of the tunnel. The next day the shunning continued. The women boiled water and prepared food, but no one would give anything to Abe, even though he was begging for water by that time.

He was seriously tempted to take some food or grab up a water bag and begin drinking. He was their captive, and they owed him food and water, but he couldn't bring himself to steal. He constantly watched the women to see where they went for water. He figured that if they got it at a spring, he could freely drink from there. But he never saw anyone walk off with empty water bags.

He made his way down to the frozen river and used a stone to chip pieces of ice to suck on. That helped his thirst a little, but he still longed for a good drink, and he was desperately hungry. It hadn't been that long since his grueling trek through the wilderness had weakened him, and he did not have the endurance he might otherwise have had.

The second morning he got up and started to walk toward the mouth of the tunnel. Three small boys had come running down the tunnel streaming wet from rain. Abe was at least going to get an adequate drink, but he had taken only three steps when he passed out.

He came to with Captain Jack leaning over him. A thin smile was on the chief's weatherbeaten face as he looked into Abe's eyes. "You are crazy, Crazy Abe," he laughed. "Why didn't you eat?"

"Because no one would give me anything," Abe answered feebly.

"Why didn't you just take the food?"

"That would have been stealing, and I do not steal."

"Humph," murmured the Indian. "Maybe so. At least, you are alive. If you had stolen food, we would have killed you."

"Why?" asked Abe. "Is it so wrong for a hungry man to want to eat?"

"No," Captain Jack laughed. "But you said you were a peace man and carried no gun because of your Jesus teachings. Hooker Jim think you lie. He say you spy for the army. I think maybe, maybe not. Maybe you are just God-crazy and not carry gun. I don't know if your God says not to carry gun, but I hear Bible in Yreka, and white man's God say no steal; I know that. Most white men not honor that, but I test you. If you steal, you not God-crazy, and we kill you. If not, maybe you are crazy. Here . . . eat." A Modoc woman handed Abe a cup of hot gruel.

"Scarfaced Charley will lead you to the road after you have eaten. You can be home for your Christmas. That's a Jesus festival, isn't it? How 'bout that?" And Captain Jack laughed.

Chapter 16

The driving sleet made it hard to talk as Scarfaced Charley led Abe out of the Lava Beds. And yet Abe had questions that needed answering.

"Captain Jack says he did not want a war. What about you?"

But Scarfaced Charley did not turn on his horse to answer.

"I heard you fired the first shot at Lost River. Is that true?" asked Abe, remembering something Davis had told him.

The Indian stopped his horse in the narrow trail and sat facing forward. Abe began to worry that he had pushed the Modoc too far. Maybe he would be angry and take Abe back to the stronghold, or worse yet, leave him in the Lava Beds to find his own way out.

Finally the Indian turned around and said, "You want to know how war start? I tell you. All Modocs want is to live in peace on Lost River, but many soldiers come. They say they take Kintpuash for killing bad medicine man. But it was just a trick to take Modocs back to Klamath Reservation. I not shoot first. Soldier start war."

"How was that?" asked Abe.

"Soldier chief tell me to lay down rifle. So I drop it, but he want my pistol too. I told him, I not shoot, but he talk to me like dog. I tell him, 'I not dog. I am man. I'm not afraid of you. You talk to me just like dog. I not dog. Talk to me good; I listen.'

"But he say, 'You dog breath. I show you.' And he shoot at me but miss. I pull pistol and shoot back. I shoot through his coat sleeve; it not hurt him. But I not shoot first. Then all soldiers shoot. Modocs run and shoot back. That how fight start.

Very bad time. White man kill women and babies."

"What?"

"White man kill women and babies. One old squaw sitting on the ground had head cut almost off by soldier sword. One baby shot out of mother's arms as she run for cover. Young girl shot dead. Two small children shot by soldier standing close enough to touch them. Only one brave killed and one hurt— just broke arm. Later, soldiers return to abandoned village and find helpless old squaw. She very old, blind, no walk. They throw many tule mats over her, make big pile. Then light on fire and burn alive."

Abe sat on his horse speechless for some time. He was shaken and appalled. Finally he said, "What about all the settlers who were killed?"

"I not do that. Kintpuash not do that. We and our braves escape, take rest of squaws and children across lake to come here. Very bad night. Canoes almost sink. Take many hours. We not kill settlers."

"Well, who did then?"

"Hooker Jim and his murderers. They not with us then. They camp on other side of Lost River. But they not kill white women and children. Only kill men."

"Well, then all you'd have to do is turn them in to the army if they're the guilty ones, and I'm sure these hostilities would be over and your people could live in peace."

Scarfaced Charley stared at Abe for a long time. "No. You Crazy Abe. You not understand. Soon we move our camp over here, near edge of lava beds to fight soldiers. It's the only way," he said. Then he kicked his horse and rode down the trail without another word.

They came to the edge of the lava flow in a few minutes. The lake was visible only a short distance ahead. Scarfaced Charley turned his horse around, passed Abe, and headed back to the Modoc camp. He didn't look up or respond in any way when Abe tried to say good-bye.

There was no point in going on to Yreka; Meacham was long gone to Washington. But the ride back to Linkville was hard on Abe, given his weakened condition. Somehow the cold, damp wind seemed to go right through his buffalo coat, and he began to shiver and sneeze. As darkness approached, he became almost too dizzy to stay in the saddle. The streets in Linkville were deserted, and Abe felt particularly lonely when he heard Christmas carols coming from one brightly lit home.

He returned his horse to the livery barn down by the lake and then made his way back to the hotel. To Abe's surprise, Davis had checked out the day before, and no one knew where he'd gone. Furthermore, there were still no vacant rooms.

Christmas Eve, and Abe had no family to share it with, not even a place to stay. A wave of dizziness hit him along with a hot flash, and he realized he was getting very sick. What a mess, he thought. His efforts to contact Meacham had failed . . . the Modocs were getting ready to renew the fight . . . everything was going wrong.

At least Mary was safe, he thought. Then he remembered that her father had been trying to get her to return to the ranch. What if she had already gone? He headed out of the hotel and over to the Widow Morgan's. He had to know.

Another dizzy spell hit him as he climbed the steps of the widow's neat house, and he had to grab a porch post to keep from losing his balance. Abe could see through the window. Inside several people were having what appeared to be a Christmas Eve party. The sight hit him hard. He felt like he had sunk to the dregs of society. Once he had lived in a nice home like this—even nicer. He'd had family, friends, and a community where people welcomed him. The idea of being alone and sick, without a place to even get in out of a storm on a Christmas Eve, would have been unimaginable to him. But here he was—filthy, wet, tired, his nose dripping so fast that he couldn't keep it wiped. He felt like a beggar.

He was about to leave, not wanting to bother decent people in his condition, when the door opened and a trim-looking army lieutenant backed out.

"Thank you, Miss Bauder. I'll be sure and tell your father. And if you don't mind, I'd be pleased to call on you tomorrow. I've got a pass to stay in Linkville overnight, it being Christmas and all."

"You'd be most welcome, Lieutenant Wright," came Mary's voice.

Abe stepped back into the shadows, hoping not to be seen, but just then the lieutenant said good-bye and turned toward him.

"Ho! What have we here? Some kind of drifter?" he said, trying to cover his surprise at Abe standing in the dark. "This can't be one of the widow's guests, can it? Be off with you."

Mary stepped out into the cold. "Who's there?"

"It's me, Mary . . . I didn't mean to interrupt your party. I was just . . ."

"Abe? Is that you . . . ?" Mary said. But her voice trailed off as the twinkling lights from the windows all dimmed to nothing.

Chapter 17

*A*be awoke to warm sunshine coming through the window, lighting a cheery little room. A cool cloth washed again and again across his forehead. He turned to see Mary sitting at the head of his bed.

"Hello, sleepyhead," she said with a little smile.

"Where . . . ?"

"At the Widow Morgan's. When you passed out, I persuaded her to put you up here in one of her rooms. She didn't want to at first . . . said this wasn't a hospital and she had no time or yen for nursin'. It wasn't until I said I'd take care of you that she agreed to have you brought up here."

"How'd you get me up here?"

"Lieutenant Wright helped me carry you up . . . after I twisted his arm a little."

"Oh, yeah . . . him," said Abe, remembering the dashing lieutenant who had been calling on Mary. "Well, thank you very much. I really didn't mean to put you to all this trouble."

He thought for a moment. "I s'pose I better be gettin' up before I waste all of Christmas day."

Mary laughed lightheartedly. "It's gone and passed you by already, Abe Miller."

"Well, not all of it," Abe said, glancing at the angle of the sun coming through the window. "It can't be much past noon yet." He started to sit up, but the room swirled and darkened so fast that he flopped back on the pillow, grabbing his head.

"I think you better stay put for a while. The doctor said you'll have quite a time recovering. Besides, there's no need to get up right now. Christmas was yesterday, and you slept straight through it with a fever high enough to boil the laundry."

"I slept through Christmas? I've been here for two nights and a whole day?"

"Yes, and I was mighty worried about you. And you still have some fever, even now." She touched his head, and then sat back looking at him, a wisp of her dark hair hanging loose across her smooth forehead. "Would you like some water? The doctor was worried that you wouldn't get enough liquid before you came around. He said a fever can drive all the moisture out of a person."

Abe rose gingerly on one elbow to sip from the cool glass she handed him. As he did, he realized that he had no clothes on at all. "Where are my clothes?" he asked, looking around the room.

"They were so filthy and wet that I had to strip them off before I put you in this nice bed of the widow's. I got 'em all washed for you. All except that buffalo hide you been wearin'. It's still hanging out in the woodshed. Once it dries, I'll take a broom to it. Maybe that'll help."

"You took my clothes off?" Abe sank back on the bed and pulled the blankets higher.

"I sure did, but the hard part was getting you from that chair there where the lieutenant dropped you, over here to the bed after I sponged you off."

Abe lay there in silence staring up at the ceiling, too embarrassed to look at Mary. He vacillated from being mortified, to telling himself that it was as natural as could be and had to be done, to feeling aroused at the thought of Mary—his beautiful Mary—touching him when he was naked.

"Abe," Mary said softly, "would you rather have had the Widow Morgan help? The lieutenant was gone, and somebody had to do it."

"Uh . . . no, no, of course not the widow," he said, trying to sound matter-of-fact, to put the whole event back in the category of necessary nursing. He was silent for a moment, then asked, "Where's Davis?"

"Davis is gone," Mary said with a touch of exasperation in her voice. "Listen, I'm sorry. I could have waited for the doctor, but he didn't come until yesterday noon, and those wet clothes were part of what was making you sick."

Hearing Mary talk in such practical terms made Abe realize that he didn't want the whole thing to be nothing but practical necessity. So he was secretly relieved when he looked over at Mary to see that she was red with embarrassment, too. Though she was talking matter-of-factly, taking care of him had meant something more to her. "Thank you, Mary," he said softly as he reached out and touched her hand. She squeezed back and smiled shyly.

A little later, Abe asked again whether Mary knew where Davis was. It turned out that when Abe did not return in a reasonable time from following Meacham, Davis got worried and took off to make the rounds of the ranches and the army encampment to see if Abe had turned up there. Mary hadn't heard from him yet, but she thought he'd be back in Linkville anytime.

It was two days before Abe's fever was gone and he could sit up in bed without feeling dizzy. Throughout that time Mary cared for him faithfully, bringing him whatever he needed. He loved to have her there but felt guilty for taking up so much of her time. Finally he said as much to her.

She blushed as she answered, "I wouldn't be here anymore than necessary if I didn't like being with you, Abe Miller."

"Well, what about that Lieutenant Wright?"

"What about him?"

"Wasn't he calling on you?"

"He came on Christmas day . . ."

"And?"

"He's a very handsome man, though somewhat of a braggart."

"What about?"

"Everything. Did you know that he's put up a serious wager of two thousand dollars that his company and one other company can whip the Modocs in fifteen minutes if they're given a chance?"

"That's impossible," said Abe. "Even if there wasn't a lick of resistance, a company couldn't even march through those Lava Beds in fifteen minutes. They're nearly impassable."

"Well, Lieutenant Wright's put up his money. From what I hear, Joe Teaney over at the saloon's holding the actual cash. A few of the locals figure to make a buck off him."

"Two thousand dollars . . . that's a lot of money. How can he afford it? Where'd he even get that much?"

"He tells everybody he's the son of General George Wright, the commander of the entire Military Division of the Pacific during the Civil War. If it's true, he'd be worth a fortune. The Wright family is very old and wealthy."

"And is he going to be seeing you some more?"

"He'd like to . . . New Year's Eve."

"And you?"

"What do you care, Abe Miller?" Mary grinned.

"I guess you know that I do care . . . started caring the first time I met you."

• • •

Jonathan Davis arrived back in town the third day after Christmas and looked up Abe. He was astounded at Abe's story about being captured and then released by the Modocs. But Davis had some troubling news. Lieutenant Colonel Frank Wheaton, commanding the District of the Lakes, had established clear plans to embark on an all-out campaign to dislodge the Modocs. And he was no flash-in-the-pan commander willing to send out a mere two companies to do the job—even if one of them was to be led by the hotshot Lieutenant Wright.

"Old Jesse Applegate's been advising Wheaton," said Davis, "and he knows this area. He says an Indian can hide in one of those cinder chimneys and shoot a man without exposing even so much as an inch of himself. Then he can reload without haste and shoot a common muzzle-loader ten times before any soldiers could scramble over the sharp rocks and chasms to get to his position. According to Applegate, if a force ever did dislodge the Indians from their cover, all they'd have to do is drop back through some ditch or tunnel and take up another ambush, equally hard to take."

"I believe he's right," said Abe. "I was in there."

"Well, Wheaton's plan is to knock out the savages with cannon and mortar fire. And that's what he's waitin' for."

"What do you mean, 'waitin' for?'"

"For his big guns to arrive. He's got a pair of twelve-pounder bronze mountain howitzers comin' in."

"How much time do we have before they arrive?" asked Abe.

"Who knows? Wheaton hoped to make his attack yesterday, on the 27th, but the guns aren't here yet. Could arrive anytime, though. Like I said, he also plans to use mortars."

Abe felt panic. The war machine was on the march, and there was no way to stop it.

That afternoon, much against Mary's advice, Abe got up and went out. He had developed a terrible cough that shook him violently whenever he exerted himself, but there was one thing he had to try and do. He had to contact Meacham by some means.

The owner of the general store was also the town mail clerk. Abe asked him if he could send a wire from town.

"The only way to do it is to write it up and have it sent down to Yreka. They can send it out from there. But it ain't cheap."

When Abe discovered the price, he decided he would just write a letter to Meacham. Meacham would be in Washington through January 6, and probably longer if Ulysses S. Grant was re-elected—which no one doubted would happen. A letter would be more confidential, and he could explain himself better.

When he got home, he set to composing his message. He worked late into the night before he was satisfied. It was a complex task to introduce himself and convince Meacham of his story. Bauder's involvement had seemed so clear, but when Abe tried to put it down on paper, it made a very thin case. From Meacham's end, it would all depend on whether he could find the official in the Indian Agency that Bauder had bribed.

If Meacham could smoke the truth out of that man, there was some hope of getting a reversal on his appointment. But, Abe wondered, what if the agent denied everything—his Indian squaw wife, Bauder's blackmail, his yielding to the extortion? These were very serious charges to make. Would Meacham have the courage and the certainty to press his case if the man denied the whole ordeal? It could be very embarrassing, and if Meacham was entering politics, he might not want to risk making enemies in Washington.

The next morning Abe's cough was much worse, and his fever had returned, but without telling Mary, he left the house early to post his letter. It was nasty and snowy out, and the exertion of merely walking to the store and back set Abe to hacking so uncontrollably that he felt weak and lightheaded.

Mary apparently heard him coughing as he entered his room, and soon she came knocking on his door. "Are you okay?"

"I think so," said Abe. "It's just this cough."

Mary stood in the doorway in her housecoat. It was the first time he had seen her with her hair down. How long and beautiful it was, rolling softly down over her shoulders in its shining black waves.

"I'm going to send for the doctor," Mary said as she heard the wheeze in Abe's labored breathing.

"I think I'll be all right."

"Well, I'm going to get him anyway. And . . . there's something else, Abe. My father is coming for me. You know he has been wanting me to return to the ranch, and Lieutenant Wright stopped by last night with word from Father that he'd be in town for me this afternoon."

"But, Mary, you can't do that! It's not safe—"

"Safe? I've lived around Indians all my life. They don't worry me."

"But how about your father?"

Mary shrugged, but the look that crossed her face was not so carefree. "We've been apart a long time, and I'm learning how to stay out of his way."

"A girl shouldn't have to stay out of her father's way. It's just not right. Look, you're a grown woman now, you don't have to do what he says. Just tell him you're not coming."

"Now how am I going to do that, Abe? Just how would I live?"

"Well, certainly you could get a job or something?"

"As what . . . a dance hall girl?"

"Of course not. You've been to college. There must be lots of jobs you could do. How about teaching school or . . . or, well at least you could be a seamstress, or something."

"Not likely," said Mary wryly. "The town already has a schoolteacher, and with all the ranch women living in town during the Indian trouble, there's plenty of extra hands for odd jobs. Besides . . . Father heard that I was nursing some man here, and I think he's got wind that it's you. I better go, but . . . you know I don't want to, don't you?"

"I don't want you to, either, Mary," Abe said as a coughing fit hit him. "If I was up and around a little more, I'd tell you that I think I'm in love with you."

Mary blushed and her tone got matter-of-fact again. "Well,

maybe it's better that you're not feeling your oats too much, then."

When the doctor arrived about noon, he listened a long time to Abe's chest. "It's pneumonia," he said. "You better plan to spend at least a couple weeks in bed, young man. This is serious, you know. Nearly one out of three people with pneumonia don't make it. Now a young man like you—in the prime of your life—ought to have better odds. But you've been putting that body of yours through quite a beating lately. Your health's not what it should be, and it's going to take some time for you to bounce back."

Abe took the news hard. The campaign against the Modocs was poised to begin . . . Mary was going back to her father's ranch, walking right into danger as hostilities broke out again . . . and Abe was too sick to respond. His only hope was for Meacham to understand and act on his letter.

Every tortured breath became a prayer.

Chapter 18

*M*ary left the next morning. Abe watched from his window as she tossed her belongings into the back of Bauder's buckboard and climbed onto the seat. Bauder did not offer her a hand, neither to help her load her belongings or mount the high seat of the buckboard. As they rolled away, Mary looked up and waved slightly with her hand.

Recovery from his pneumonia was slow and tedious for Abe. Davis settled up with Mrs. Morgan for Abe's room and board. From time to time he brought his sick friend the things he needed and reported regularly on developments with the Modocs.

"Colonel Wheaton finally got his howitzers," Davis said one day in the middle of January. "More reinforcements too and new arms. Looks like they're ready to go anytime now. They say he's got about 350 men, enough to make mincemeat of the whole tribe."

"Has there been any word from Meacham?" Abe asked anxiously, his voice wheezing.

"Not as of yesterday, but I'll check again today. You'd think he could wire or something by now . . . if he got your message at all, that is."

Two days later, when there still was no word from Meacham, Abe got up. "I'm going down to the army camp," he told Davis. "I've got to see if there's something I can do to forestall this attack. Will you go with me?"

"I don't know, Abe," Davis said, pulling at the edge of his big mustache. "I'm not sure it's a good idea to go down there.

What in blazes do you think you can do?"

"I don't know . . . I've got to do something! It's going to be a slaughter. Maybe I should tell Wheaton about what Bauder's done. Maybe he'll listen."

"But you don't have any proof—not real proof anyway. The proof's in Washington. Without it, and without Meacham's hopefully sympathetic ear, you'll get nowhere. Besides, I've heard that Bauder and several local settlers are working closely with the army as a kind of volunteer militia. Bauder's their leader. He and Wheaton have to be pretty tight. You'll get nowhere."

"But I've got to try," Abe said stubbornly. "You said yourself that Wheaton is about to begin his offensive. With those big guns, he'll crush the Modocs for sure."

"But Abe, if you tip your hand early—without the proof Meacham can provide—you'll only give Bauder the opportunity to defend himself."

"But waiting for Meacham may be too late! You with me or not?"

Davis threw up his hands. "Well, all right. But don't say I didn't warn you!"

• • •

Abe and Jonathan were over halfway to the army camp at Lost River the next day when they met a man riding hard going north. He pulled up when he came abreast.

"George Ramsey, from the *Oregonian*," he announced importantly. "Fightin's started. We're whippin' the tar out of 'em . . . I think. But those Indians could scatter anytime and end up running all over the country. Gotta wire in my story." He spurred his horse and was gone.

Davis snorted. "Ha. He doesn't really know a thing, does he?" he said as they watched the man ride away.

Abe and Jonathan kicked their livery horses into a fast trot.

When they arrived at the Lost River camp, it was only manned by a small defensive force. The quick word was that fighting was heavy, but the army hadn't used its mortars and howitzers. "One of those strange fogs moved in from the Lava Beds," said a guard. "Seems the spotters can't see where the rounds are hitting, so they can't adjust their fire."

Davis slipped the guard a silver dollar to allow them to change horses with a couple nags still at camp. "Don't worry, we'll bring 'em back. And if we don't, you got our horses, and they're twice as good as these sorry beasts."

As they rode around the west side of the lake toward its south tip, they could see the fog bank in the otherwise bright afternoon. It undulated like a dark curtain at the end of the world. As they rode into it, the damp mist penetrated to their skin, and there was a strange smell of sulfur to the air. Finally they could hear the muffled popping of small arms fire. But the fog that prevented them from seeing more than twenty yards ahead also confused all direction to sound.

"What if we wander right into the battle?" worried Abe.

"I just hope that guard knew what he was talking about. Captain Jack's stronghold is supposed to be at the very south end of the lake. If the army went down the west side of the lake, like we're doing, then it has to be between us and the battlefield. But if they set up headquarters somewhere else, who knows where the fighting is happening."

"Who goes there?" challenged a ghostly voice out of the fog.

"Don't shoot! . . . It's Jonathan Davis."

"And Abraham Miller. We're comin' in, okay?"

In the field camp, they found a wounded captain eager to tell about the battle. "Name's Nat Baswick. I was the first one to get hit. Felt like a fool writhin' around on the ground."

"How'd it start?" asked Abe, frowning.

"Last night the boys were all charged up, talking about how they was gonna have Modoc steak for dinner today and who wanted it raw and who wanted it roasted. There was no stoppin' 'em. But sometime after midnight one of the guards started shooting and screaming—woke up everyone. Turns out he was shooting at his moon shadow or something, but it sure unnerved everyone.

"This morning when we set out to make our assault, there wasn't an Injun in sight. That got everyone goin' again, real anxious like. They were saying stuff like, 'I knew them red devils would run when they learned we were after 'em,' and then they began to chant, 'We want Injuns . . . we want Injuns . . . show us Injuns, and we'll show you some dead ones.'"

Davis and Abe looked at each other.

"But after getting all set in formation," Baswick went on, "we advanced no more than fifty yards when a shot rang out, and I flopped down on the ground, my thigh broken with a slug right through it. Everybody just stood there till I yelled, 'Unfetter yourselves, you fools; can't you see I've been shot? Get me to some cover!'

"They moved then. Got me behind a pile of rocks and splinted up my leg. Then the Indians opened up. Seemed like they were everywhere and nowhere. It was all confusion for a time. Then Wheaton, who was back with the artillery, cut loose with his mortars and howitzers. But he didn't even have time to sight in before this bank of fog you see came rolling in. Came right out of them Lava Beds like the wall of water that drowned Pharaoh's army.

"So Wheaton had to shut down his guns. As it was, a couple mortar rounds landed among some of those civilian volunteers who were with us. We fired volley after volley into those rocks, but I don't think anyone saw the enemy."

The wounded man winced, but seemed eager to replay the battle. "About noon, the fog lifted for a few minutes. Everyone cheered, and the bugle called charge. I could see everything at that point. They all jumped up and started running across the flat, fully exposed. The Indians kept up a withering fire on them. Men were dropping everywhere. I still didn't see any

Indians. The most you could see were occasional puffs of smoke from where they were shooting.

"Then the fog came back down, and our boys started carrying back the wounded. Just look around you. More than fifty men killed or wounded. Finally the whole army retreated back here to camp and set up defensive positions."

Baswick shook his head. "One of the worst things is that a lot of the boys lost their weapons and ammunition out there. Those Injuns are probably harvestin' 'em right now. I mean brand new carbines and Henry's and belts plum full of cartridges. In fact, there's a whole case of ammunition missing somewhere. More'n likely it's in Captain Jack's stronghold by now. When them fickle volunteers hightailed it, half of them left Spencers, Remingtons, and Ballards on the field, too."

"What's your complaint about the volunteers?" a voice from behind boomed.

Abe looked around to see Bauder stagger up. Dirt and blood covered him, but apparently he was uninjured.

"I was just saying that half your boys left their rifles out there for the Modocs," groused the captain.

"You wanna make somethin' of it?"

"No. I just don't relish facing an enemy that's better armed than we are, especially if we did the arming."

"Doesn't look to me like you'll have to face anyone, seein's how you got yourself shot. And what're you doin' here, Miller?" snapped Bauder.

Abe just stared at him. What could he say?

"Go back East where you belong, you coward. And I thought I told you to stay away from my Mary. You understand?"

"I think she's old enough to make her own decisions," Abe ventured.

"Yeah? Well, I guess I'm old enough to make my own decisions, too," Bauder sneered. "And I've decided to break your head if you don't keep your nose out of other people's business."

Abe felt his blood boil. "Bauder, you don't scare me. I'll see her if and when she wants to see me."

Bauder's jaw muscles pulsed. But before he could answer, someone yelled, "Injuns! Injuns comin' in!" The alarm came from several soldiers huddled around a fire they'd built to take the chill off the damp evening.

"Get away from that bloomin' fire and take cover," yelled Bauder as he drew his pistol and dove behind a pile of rocks. Abe and Jonathan dropped where they were beside the wounded Captain Baswick.

Someone fired a shot, and then from out of the gloom they heard a feeble shout. "No shoot! No shoot me!"

It was one of the Klamath scouts who had been working with the army. He and a second scout had been captured by the Modocs. This one had no idea what happened to his partner, but the Modocs released him . . . after they "taught him a lesson."

He was stark naked, and his feet were badly cut from walking through the sharp Lava Beds. The Klamath also had great welts all over his buttocks, legs, and back as though he had been whipped mercilessly with reeds or willows. Blood oozed down over his left eye from a scalp wound.

The soldiers stood up and backed away as the Indian scout staggered toward the fire. Finally, after he had stared into the blaze for several moments, someone spoke up: "Here, give the lad some water." Someone produced a canteen, and the spell was broken.

As they plied the Klamath with questions, he reported that the Modocs were having a great celebration. Not only had they driven off the blue coats, but—as had been suspected—they had salvaged dozens of the finest weapons from the field, plus hundreds of rounds of ammunition.

"How many of them devils did we get?" asked a soldier.

"They not lose any braves."

"You mean we didn't kill one Modoc?"

"No Modocs dead . . . no Modocs wounded."

"How do you know?" said the angry voice. "Maybe they were off in a cave somewhere, and you couldn't see 'em."

The Klamath shook his head. "They had big war dance. Each brave jump out when his name was sung and count coup on me." He indicated the welts all over his body. "No one missing."

Chapter 19

*T*he next morning Colonel Wheaton received orders from General Gillem to withdraw the company and report to his headquarters at Fairchild's ranch. The dead received a temporary burial. The wounded that couldn't walk were loaded on wagons or hand-carried litters, and the field camp was abandoned.

Bauder and the volunteers left for Linkville. Jonathan Davis decided to go with them.

"I think I'll be staying here for a little while," Abe told him.

"You'll what?"

"You go ahead. I'll be along later today."

"You'll do no such thing. If you hang around here by yourself, those Modocs are liable to capture you."

Abe grimaced. "It wouldn't be the first time."

"I know. But they're on the warpath now. They've had a big swig of blood; they'll want more."

"I doubt they want mine."

"Well, I'm not staying with you, if that's what you're thinking."

"Wouldn't want you to. I'll be safer by myself. Besides, I need to be alone for a while."

"What's that you said the Modocs called you? Crazy Abe? Well, they sure had it right. You're plum loco." Davis shook his head. "You know, Miller, you're fighting so hard that one of these days you're liable to find yourself fighting the Almighty Himself."

"Come on, Davis. You're not suggestin' that it's God's idea

for these Indians to be driven off their land."

"No, no. That's entirely the work of Bauder and his bunch."

"Then in working against Bauder, how could I possibly be fighting God?"

"Maybe . . ." Davis looked off across the Lava Beds and then back at his friend. "Maybe when you're trying to be God."

"'Be God'? That's ridiculous—"

"Of course it is," Davis interrupted, "and that's my point. God has the uncomfortable habit of letting people do evil deeds if they're determined to do so. Though He disapproves, He doesn't force 'em to be good. But not Abe Miller. Oh, no. You gotta get in there and make 'em do right . . . that's when it seems you're trying to be God."

"Hey, I'm not trying to be God," Abe shot back. "I'm just trying to do what's right myself. If we all did that, Bauder would have to go along. Remember? You were the one who told me on the train that civilization constrained characters like Bauder. Well, I'm just doing my part keeping civilization alive."

"No you're not. You have very little respect for the social order."

Abe looked startled. "Well, maybe not . . . maybe not. But that's because it's corrupt. How can I respect it? Whether the army admits it or not, it's doin' Bauder's dirty work."

"Look, all I'm trying to say," said Davis as he swung up onto his horse, "is, when you can't influence people to do what you think is right, don't resort to forcing it on 'em. Leave that to God, and don't be surprised when He doesn't force 'em either . . . though at some point they'll face the consequences."

"I suppose," said Abe without much conviction.

"Hey, you comin'? Let's get out of here. This place gives me the creeps."

"No. You go on."

"Well, it's your funeral," Davis shrugged. "Fact is, we may never find your body to give it a funeral."

Abe slapped Davis' horse on the rump, and it loped off to

catch up with the volunteers.

The bright sun had almost chased the chill from the winter morning. A magpie's squawk broke the silence as it swooped down to search for food among scraps the men had left around their smoldering fires. Its sharply sculpted black and white body made it the policeman of the wilderness. Abe walked through the deserted camp. Gone without a trace was the eerie fog. Gone were the tents, the cannons, the hundreds of men. Gone, too, were the moans of the wounded that had tormented Abe's night's sleep.

Soon there wouldn't be a trace of the death and destruction that had flooded over this peaceful plain the day before. How quickly it would be forgotten. But as Abe wandered out over the battlefield, he realized this wasn't quite true. Here and there he spied spent cartridges, a torn and bloody coat, an old rag, a boot, a canteen with a bullet hole through it.

He eyed the small hill ahead of him to the southeast where Captain Jack's stronghold supposedly was, but he never saw any Indians, though once he thought a wisp of smoke rose from the rocks. But when he blinked, it was gone.

On his left glimmered Tule Lake in the morning sun. Three killdeers called each other plaintively by name as they raced back and forth on the mudflat at the water's edge. Engrossed in the peace of the place, Abe stumbled and almost fell as he came over a small rise. Up leaped three black monsters, beating the air with huge fans as they fought to take wing. Vultures! Abe smelled death—not the penetrating stench of the long dead, but the subtle, nauseating spice of the recently deceased that reached out to grab his soul. Abe knew that smell well! The whiff had come just before finding each of his family members in the collapsed house. And there, behind some sagebrush, was an Indian, his eyes pecked out, his gut raked open and picked over. His genitals . . . gone.

Abe fell back to the ground. He stared at the man. Dried blood encrusted his feet. There were slight marks on his legs.

He must be the other Klamath scout, Abe thought. Then he began to sob. The sobs came deeper and deeper; he didn't know why. This Indian didn't mean a thing to him personally. He'd never even seen the man before.

After a time, he got control of himself. Wiping his nose on his sleeve, he got up and tried to figure what to do with the body. For some reason, he just couldn't pick up the mutilated body to carry it back to the other temporary graves. But he had nothing with which to dig a grave, so he decided to cover the body with stones. When he finished, he found the trunk of a small, dead juniper tree and erected it as a marker. He thought about using some item of discarded clothing from the battle-field to tie a crosspiece to the pole and make a cross. But why? Instead, he hung the shot-up canteen from the top of the pole so it would be visible should anyone want to retrieve the body.

Then Abe returned to his horse and rode north.

• • •

On his way back to Linkville, Abe considered stopping by the Bauder ranch along Lost River. He wanted to get his mind off the killing . . . off the wasteland of the battlefield. A visit with Mary would lift his spirits. And if Bauder had done what he said he was going to do, he would be miles north on his way to Linkville for a strategy meeting.

Abe had never been to the ranch before, but from Mary's description, he had a good idea where to find it. He wanted to see her. It had been a couple weeks already. He could talk to her and sort out what he should do if Meacham didn't return.

When Abe rode up the lane toward the ranch house, Mary was replacing some broken shakes on the east eaves where a dead limb from one of the tall pines had fallen. Abe had to admit that it was a beautiful home, built of logs and well chinked. He could see a huge fireplace on the south end, another stone chimney on the other end, and a stovepipe rising from the back of the house. Whispering pines set the ranch off from the surrounding countryside, as though generations ago someone had planted them just for Bauder.

Abe dismounted his horse quietly as he watched Mary finish her task. She was a remarkable woman—beautiful as a queen and yet strong and capable enough to be a man's real partner and companion.

Suddenly he realized Mary was just the kind of woman he'd like to marry. Marriage . . . yes! He'd like to marry Mary Bauder. It surprised him that he hadn't known it before—it seemed so obvious. He'd known he was in love with her, and had allowed himself to daydream what it would be like to marry her. But he had never contemplated marriage to her as a real goal. But then, maybe it wasn't possible, he smiled wryly to himself. After all, it takes two to agree on such a thing. A chill struck Abe as he realized there was a good chance she wouldn't be interested.

In spite of her long dress, she was climbing down the ladder as nimbly as a deer when Abe called out, "Hello, Mary."

She whirled. "Oh, Abe, you startled me. I didn't know anyone was around. You're looking better. How do you feel?"

"About normal, though I get winded sometimes."

"What are you doing down here?"

They stood on the veranda as Abe told about hearing that Colonel Wheaton was about to invade the Lava Beds and how he'd hoped to try and talk him out of it—only to arrive too late.

"Yes. I thought I heard the booming of guns yesterday afternoon . . . Oh, Abe, I'm worried. I'm afraid the way you're going about this is just going to lead to more trouble."

"What do you want me to do? I'm not the kind of guy who walks away from trouble, you know."

"No, but you are the kind of guy who takes on trouble that's not your own."

Abe stared awkwardly. "Yeah, well, if everyone just minded their own business, the Modocs would be wiped out before spring."

"I'm not saying you shouldn't help, Abe," Mary said gently. "But there's a time and place for things, and right now I think there are ways you could help that would be more your part . . . more your size."

That stung. Was it true? Or did Mary not respect him? Abe wasn't sure, so he tried to laugh it off. "Now you sound like Davis. He thinks I'm playin' God. But Mary, listen . . . I can't just sit back and let this war go on. I don't have to be elected president or commissioned a general to have the authority to do what's morally right, do I?" For a few moments Abe was lost in his thoughts. Then he added, "Maybe when Meacham gets here . . . he's official, maybe he can get this whole tragedy turned around."

"I hope so. He had a much better way with the Indians than Odeneal. But even Meacham didn't have much luck keeping the Modocs on the reservation."

"That's because the government put them on the Klamath reservation where they were bottom dogs! I should hope Meacham now sees that some other arrangement must be found. Of course, there's not much chance in convincing Odeneal of that."

"No, there's not. He's about like my father. He'd rather they were dead. Speaking of my father . . ." Mary looked a little anxious. ". . . he wouldn't be very happy to find you here."

"I know, but he's gone up to Linkville. I doubt that he'll be back this afternoon."

"Well, come on in then. I'll get you some coffee."

"Thanks."

Inside, the house was as spacious as it appeared from without. There were three windows facing west with a beautiful view of Lost River below. And in the kitchen, there was even an indoor pump.

Abe lowered his lanky frame into a kitchen chair. "You know, it's pretty hard to see much of you the way your father feels about me. He got all over me again last night. Told me he didn't want me seeing you anymore."

"I know. But that might change. I'm hoping to get a job at the bank in Linkville. If I do, I'll be moving up there." She smiled.

"Mary! That'd be wonderful. When?"

"I don't know. They've never had a woman work in the bank before, so I've had to convince them that I can do the job—that I can count, add, subtract, and write letters." She put a cup of steaming coffee before Abe and sat across from him. "It's really the kind of stuff any school kid could do."

"What's happening? Is the bank expanding or something?"

"I don't think that's it, so much. There are a lot more people in town right now because of the Indian trouble and all. But the real opening is because old man Beckman has had a stroke or something. He still comes in to the bank some, but he can't really write anymore, and even his speech is hard for people to understand. So, his brother is looking for someone to help out."

"That's wonderful, Mary, and I'm just as glad that you're getting away from your father. I wouldn't trust him if I were you."

Mary looked away with a frown as though Abe had brought up something she'd rather not think about, but she responded. "I never used to feel that way when Momma was alive, but since I came back from school . . . he—he seems so different now."

"If he ever hits you," injected Abe, "you just let me know. I'll—"

"Abe." Mary put a hand on his arm. "He hasn't—I've warned him—at least, not since that time on the train when you first saw us." She paused. "I-I've tried not to cross him or argue with him. But . . . he does scare me when he goes off in one of his rages . . . "

"So much more a reason to move to Linkville. At least there you'll be out of harm's way."

"Yes," Mary said with a sigh as she turned away. "I did feel safer when I was living with the Widow Morgan."

"Say, do you suppose that maybe when you move to town . . . ? Well, I've been thinkin'—'bout us and all . . . What I'm trying to say, Mary, is would you consider—?"

"Abe." She stepped toward him. "When I move to town—if I move to town—I'd be glad to see you sometimes. I really would. I like you, Abraham Miller. In fact, I like you so much that I don't want you to have a run-in with my father should he end up coming home this afternoon, so you better be on your way. Besides, it's getting kind of late if you're going to make it to Linkville before dark. As it is, you might meet him on the way."

"Yeah . . . guess I'd better be goin'." Abe gulped down the last of his coffee and stood up. She liked him, she really liked him—but what did that mean? He turned and strode toward the door, grabbed his hat from the hook and put it on. "Mary—" he said as he turned, and there she was standing right behind him. Before the moment passed and without letting himself think twice, he wrapped his arms around her slim waist and kissed her on the lips.

"You better go, Abe," she whispered, gently pushing him away. Her face flushed as she opened the door.

Abe rode the two hours to Linkville in a delicious daze.

• • •

For the Modocs, events turned for the better on January 30. On that crackling cold day, Alfred B. Meacham came riding into Linkville. Better still, he brought with him a directive from President Ulysses S. Grant designating him as the chairman of a Peace Commission. All hostilities were to be suspended (except defensive actions) while Meacham gathered a Peace Commission to settle the dispute without further bloodshed.

Abe was beside himself with excitement when he heard the news, and went directly to George Nurse's hotel first thing in the morning to meet Meacham. He found him in the tiny lobby surrounded by several townspeople who were greeting Meacham, asking how his service on the Electoral College in Washington, D.C. had gone and wanting to know about the Peace Commission. Meacham was a solidly built, middle-aged man with piercing, dark eyes. Gray lamb-chop sideburns, connected by a full mustache, enhanced his heavy, square jaw. To Abe, his balding head purported virile power rather than any weakness of age.

"Mr. Meacham!" Abe said over the hubbub. "Mr. Meacham, I'm Abraham Miller. I take it you got my letter, and I'm so glad you're here." Meacham ignored him and went on talking to someone else. Abe tried again. "Mr. Meacham, I'm Abraham Miller. Did you get my letter? What did you discover?"

Suddenly, Meacham turned on Abe and in a booming voice said, "Young man, I have never met you, and I do not have time to get to know you now. Please do not interrupt me."

"But . . . did Bauder get to Kramer like I said?"

But Meacham was already striding out of the hotel. Abe followed him out onto the porch and watched as the solitary figure headed toward the livery.

Abe was dumbfounded. What was going on? Here was the one person who had a chance to end the hostilities, but he wouldn't even acknowledge Abe's presence. Confused, Abe followed Meacham down to Manning's livery barn. The livery was not much more than a public barn with stalls for about thirty horses. No one was on regular duty; each person just paid George Nurse for stable space and feed or to rent a horse as needed.

In the dark shadows of the barn, Abe approached Meacham cautiously. The agent stopped currying his horse and stepped around to offer his hand. "Mr. Miller, please forgive me for the rude way I behaved back there." He walked quickly to the door and looked up and down the street, then returned. "I'm sorry, but I couldn't let anyone know that I knew who you were."

"What do you mean?"

"I've come back with the authority of the President of the United States to try and settle this uprising without anymore killing. But there's not going to be a lasting peace around here if Reno Bauder is so determined that he'll start a war just to get the Modocs off Lost River."

"Then you've got to do something to stop him," urged Abe. "Can't you have him arrested for blackmail?"

"You were probably right about Bauder blackmailing Kramer to get me replaced by Odeneal . . . but Kramer wouldn't admit it, so I can't bring any charges against Bauder. The most I can hope for is to watch him closely . . . maybe he'll make a slip out here. Then I can nail him. That's why I didn't want to acknowledge you back in the hotel. The gossip grapevine around here is as fast as the telegraph. You were asking direct questions about the situation that would have let people know the whole story—at least, as we suspect it. Bauder would soon find out and watch himself so we couldn't do anything."

"Yes . . . yes, I see what you mean. Sorry to press you so hard," apologized Abe.

"That's okay. But from now on, don't breathe a word to anyone about our suspicions. Bauder mustn't learn that you wrote me or that we know about the blackmail. At this point, I have plenty of authority to suspend any offensive moves against the Modocs while we try to achieve peace. In the meantime, we'll keep an eye on Bauder."

Abe smiled to himself as he headed back to the hotel for some breakfast. He'd be watching Bauder, all right.

Chapter 20

*A*be was walking back to the Widow Morgan's after breakfast when a young trooper rode up beside the boardwalk and said, "Are you the fellow Captain Jack captured a few weeks ago?"

"That's right."

"I thought I recognized you." The trooper's horse blew hard and hung its head. It was lathered about the neck and withers. "I was with Lieutenant Wright at the Widow Morgan's on Christmas Eve, the night you came in looking like a drowned rat. Collapsed right there on the porch, as I recall."

"Guess I did," admitted Abe.

"Well, I've been ridin' most of the night—was sent to fetch you to Fort Klamath. General Canby just arrived, and he wants to see you . . . Abraham Miller, right?"

Abe nodded. "Who's General Canby?"

"You don't know who General Edward Richard Sprigg Canby is?" drawled the soldier as he dismounted. "He's the brigadier general of the Department of the Columbia, and he came all the way down here from Portland to straighten out this mess with the Modocs."

"But . . . uh . . . I heard Alfred Meacham just arrived here with orders from President Grant to set up a Peace Commission to settle the dispute—without any more fighting."

The trooper shrugged. "I don't know about any Meacham. But as brigadier general, Canby is the army commander over any Indian problem in the whole northwestern part for these here United States of America—and he's asking for you."

Abe felt a twinge of caution. Was this General Canby going to launch another battle—just when the hope for peace was at hand?

"What's he want with me? It's a long way round the lake up to Fort Klamath."

"Intelligence, man—and communications. You were the last white man inside Captain Jack's camp. You talked to that redskin, so General Canby thinks Jack might trust you."

Abe made a wry face. "I doubt it. He calls me 'Crazy Abe'..."

"But he didn't kill you."

"No, but—"

"Then let's go. You might be gone for a few days, so get whatever you need. I'll find a fresh horse and grab some coffee at Nurse's, but be ready to leave in half an hour."

What could it hurt? Abe thought. Maybe he could pick up some useful information on what the army was thinking. He left word for Davis at the hotel that he was heading for Fort Klamath. On second thought, he also scribbled a hurried note to Meacham.

It was almost dusk when the two men rode into Fort Klamath. The soldier took Abe straight to Canby's office. Two desks were the only furniture; behind one sat the general studying some papers, and in the corner a sergeant sat writing at the other. Each desk had an oil lamp and a third lamp hung by the door. No drapes covered the two windows. A flag stood in one corner, two benches were parked on either side of the door, and a large map covered the wall behind the general. Otherwise the room was bare.

Abe took off his hat and twirled it nervously in his hands as he stood in front of the general's desk. The general looked up from his papers. "Hello . . . Miller is it?"

Abe nodded, staring into the man's mild eyes and pleasant face. He didn't look like some war-hardened killer.

"You from around these parts?" the general asked.

"No sir. I come from Indiana."

"You don't say?" grinned the general. "That's my home state. I was born in Kentucky, but I grew up in Indiana, so I consider it my home. What part you from?"

"Northwest . . . near Goshen."

"I know it well, know it well. You wouldn't be Amish, would you?"

"No . . . Mennonite."

"I thought you were one or the other." Then, while pointing to Abe, he turned to his aide and said, "No finer people, these Mennonites. They're the most God-fearing folks on the face of this earth.

"Now," he said to Abe while he shuffled the papers in front of him, "tomorrow I'm going down to Tule Lake where this rag-tag army of mine is camped and see if we can't get this thing straightened out with those Modocs. Got word from Washington that this dispute's to be settled peacefully, which suits me fine, 'cause I don't have any interest in killing Indians—whether they're renegades or not."

The general sat back and studied Abe. "I suppose you've heard of Alfred Meacham? Well, he and I and a preacher—a reverend named Elesar Thomas, a Methodist minister from San Francisco—have been appointed as the Peace Commission to settle this mess."

Abe's ears perked up. So Canby was on the Peace Commission, too!

"What I want you for, young man, is to tell me everything you can about this chief, this Captain Jack. I understand you were held inside his camp a few weeks ago."

"That's right," said Abe.

"'Captain Jack,' huh," said the general rubbing his chin. "Did you happen to learn his Indian name?"

"Yes, it's Kintpuash, but everyone calls him 'Captain Jack.'"

"He doesn't mind going by a white name?"

Abe shrugged. "I don't think so. He likes to wear old army clothes. 'Captain' seems to suit him fine."

"Do you think there's any chance of your getting back in there and out again without losing your scalp?"

"You mean spy for you?" Abe shook his head. "I don't—"

"No, no, no. I mean take messages to him; arrange a parley; help us set up a peace council with the chief. I've got to have somebody he'll trust."

"Well, I don't know whether he trusts me in that sort of way, or not. As I told the trooper on the way out here, Captain Jack calls me 'Crazy Abe.' That doesn't suggest much confidence."

"'Crazy Abe,' huh? Now tell me why he calls you that." Canby squinted at Abe and leaned forward.

Abe felt a little awkward, but he told the general how Captain Jack just couldn't believe he wasn't carrying a gun. "They didn't give me anything to eat for a few days—some kind of test. When I didn't steal food from them, they decided I must be crazy. I guess they figured that if I was crazy enough not to steal their food, maybe I was crazy enough not to carry a gun on the trail. So . . . they believed me."

"Perfect!" concluded the general as he clapped his hands together. "He's convinced you are guileless. I'm embarrassed to admit it, Miller, but the Indians have been betrayed so often by the white man, that they suspect our every gesture. The biggest problem I have in settling these little uprisings is that I can't get the Indians to trust anyone. But with you"—he pointed a finger at Abe—"we've got a place to start. Of course, you know that it only serves the cause of peace for you to keep your eyes open whenever you are with those Indians and let me know if there's any hint of them getting ready to mobilize against us. We can't allow them to surprise us. You don't have any problem with that, do you? It's part of keeping the peace."

"I guess not."

"Good. Then I take it you're ready to enlist?"

"Enlist? Well, sir, I'm not really a military kind of person. You see, we Mennonites don't believe—"

"I know, I know. It was just a manner of speaking. I wouldn't want you wearing blues, anyway. That'd ruin the whole thing. I meant, are you ready to help us . . . for the sake of peace and all?"

"Of course," said Abe. "That's why I'm out here. For peace. By the way, maybe you can straighten things out with—"

"Good," interrupted the general. "I want you to go down there with me tomorrow. On the way, you can tell me everything you know about Captain Jack—what he's like, how his people are, how many braves he has, how they're armed . . . everything." He turned. "Sergeant, take this young man and find him a bunk. See you in the morning, Miller."

• • •

The next day when they arrived at field headquarters set up at the Fairchild's ranch south of the Lost River camp, General Canby introduced Abe to Reverend Elesar Thomas and Alfred Meacham who had preceded them. "I'm hoping to use Abe Miller to contact Captain Jack so we can set up this peace council you've got planned, Meacham."

"Hello, Mr. Miller," said Meacham. "I think I recall seeing you in Linkville the other day, but I'm glad to be formally introduced to you now."

Okay, I'll go along with the charade, Abe thought, extending his hand. "How do you do, Mr. Meacham?"

"Abe, Meacham here is the head of our illustrious Peace Commission. We've known each other for several years. He's a good man, though I thought I'd lost him recently when he went back to Washington. What happened, anyway, Meach? First you were the Indian superintendent, and now it's this Odeneal fellow."

Meacham smiled faintly. "I'll tell you all about it sometime, General."

• • •

Two days later General Canby summoned Abe. A young Indian woman was with the general. "Miller, this is Winema. She's Modoc and married to a local white man named Frank Riddle. She's eager to achieve peace for her people and can help you anytime you need a translator." Turning to the Indian woman, he said, "You're actually kin of some sort to Captain Jack, aren't you, Winema?"

"He's my father's brother's son."

"Father's brother's son . . . that makes you cousins. Good. So, you see, Miller, she should have some 'in' with him, too. I want John Fairchild to go with you, as well. He's one of the few settlers around here who has maintained a good relationship with the Modocs."

Abe nodded, and by noon the three were on their way.

Two Modoc scouts met them at the edge of the Lava Beds and told them to dismount. One took their horses, and the other led the emissaries into the Indian camp. Abe could see why Captain Jack had changed his location. By moving to the northern edge of the Lava Beds, he had easy access to the lake while behind him lay miles and miles of naturally occurring fortifications to which he could fall back if he were hard pressed. But why that would ever be necessary, Abe couldn't imagine. The Indian's forward stronghold looked utterly impregnable.

It was situated on a slight hill where in some ancient time the earth had spewed forth molten lava. As the lava cooled it cracked, creating substantial trenches that roughly followed the contour of the crown of the hill. The outer edges of this lava made a stone palisade about shoulder high with periodic cracks and portholes ideally designed for shooting through. Where this natural bulwark was incomplete, the Modocs only needed to pile a few stones to create a perfect wall. The Modocs could run through these trenches to resupply one another or shift their fire from one side to the other as needed—all without ever exposing themselves.

Add to this, numerous "outpost" lava chimneys from which a man could fight all day without being hit and other deep fissures and ravines that led back into the Lava Beds allowing for a safe retrograde maneuver, and Captain Jack had the perfect defensive stronghold.

It was down a path through one of these fissures that the scout led the envoy until they came to a small basin. This was the Indian's camp, with much evidence of domestic life: make-shift shelters, women and children running to and fro, piles of brush for firewood, baskets, bones from past meals, and other scattered items. On one side was a cave in the rock wall. From it stepped Captain Jack, Scarfaced Charley, and several other braves.

"What you want here?" challenged Jack.

"We're here to have a good talk with you," said Winema. "We plan to stay the night, so we'll tell you everything around the fire."

"You might stay longer than you want," laughed Scarfaced Charley. "Winema, you know we've been fighting the whites, and we not quit yet. We might just keep you."

"Charley, I know what you say, but listen, these men are your friends, and I am a Modoc. That's why we come among you—to help you. We know you will not harm us."

"Then you know too much." Scarfaced Charley turned and walked away.

Captain Jack motioned to a boy who ran off across the camp. From where Abe stood, he could not see a break in the wall enclosing that side of the camp, and yet a short while later, Abe looked up to see the boy returning, leading their horses across the camp and out through a more obvious passage. Then a woman handed them some dried meat.

Jack turned and took Abe and his companions into the cave. Abe noted it was nothing like the spacious caves of their former camp. This was a small hollow with a low sloping ceiling, preventing most men from standing erect except near the front. Part of the ceiling had caved in creating a heap of rock in the middle of the floor. Acrid smoke curled from a small fire pit near the back. Captain Jack took his seat on a dusty, old deerskin near the fire. Abe, Winema, and Fairchild located themselves across from him as a couple dozen braves squeezed into the cave. Some stooped down on their haunches, some sat in the dust, and some stood, but all had their guns.

Abe shifted his position, but there was nothing soft or comfortable in the Lava Beds. After sitting silently for a while, he ventured: "Captain Jack, we come here as your friends. We didn't bring any guns or pistols. We don't need them because we trust you."

"Ha! You just Crazy Abe. You don't have gun even when you need one."

"Maybe not, but now we place all our confidence in you."

"Don't worry. We won't harm you. I do not take life when not necessary. Life is sweet. I only kill in self-defense—if I can." Jack stopped and stared into the embers of the dying fire. "I know all my people are doomed. I cannot hold out long in these rocks against so many soldiers. More keep coming."

At that moment Scarfaced Charley pushed his way through the others and took a seat slightly behind Captain Jack. Then the chief continued as he looked at the two white men, "I know you come here to make offer, but I can't promise anything."

Then Fairchild said, "We're not here to make offers. We've come to invite you to a council where you can hear what the Great Father in Washington wants to do for the Modocs."

"All we want is our home on Lost River."

"We know that," continued Fairchild, "but you must talk to the Peace Commission, General Canby, Alfred Meacham—you all know him—and Reverend Thomas, a man of God. They are good men; they won't lead your people into trouble."

"Meacham come back?" asked Scarfaced Charley.

"Yes," said Abe. "He came back a few days ago."

"Will he be Indian agent now?"

"No, but he does have orders from the Great Father in Washington that there is to be no more fighting, only peace."

"But will we get our home back?" pressed Captain Jack.

"We don't know," said Abe. "But I'm sure you can work out something."

"Why should we have big talk if we don't get home?"

"Listen," said Abe, "I'm sorry your people have so much trouble, but trouble happens all over the world. There are thousands of people who have been at war but now live in peace. The way they did this was to have councils. The leading men from both sides talked over their troubles and made peace. They quit fighting. You can do the same."

"Even though we killed white men?"

"Yes. If you will listen to the government men sent here to make peace with you, you will be safe and treated right. The men the government sent to talk to you are at John Fairchild's ranch right now. They want to talk. The soldiers won't hurt you if you talk peace."

Jack sat unmoving for a long time. Then he threw a twig into the ashes. "All right. You go back and tell them that I will hear them in council and see what they offer me and my people. Tell them to come see me anytime."

"Just a moment, Jack," said Winema. "I don't think that will work. I don't think they would want to come here."

"No worry. We not harm them at talks. They be safe."

"All the same, you should go to them. After all, these two white men already made the first move by coming here to see you. Now it is your turn."

Scarfaced Charley shook his head. "Don't go. It trap."

"No, it's not a trap," urged John Fairchild. "You come to my house. You know my house. You've always been welcome there. You'll be safe at my place. I guarantee that."

"How many soldiers?" asked Captain Jack.

"Not many. I'll send most of them away. It's my place; I'll get rid of most of them. You'll be safe."

The chief looked around the cave at his braves. "I will go and see if they protect me from my enemies while we have these peace councils. Tell them that I am willing to hear anything they have to offer, if it is reasonable."

"Thank you, Captain Jack. You'll not regret this day," said Abe, thrusting out his hand. But the Indian did not shake it.

• • •

Weeks passed but the Peace Commission and the Modocs had not been able to agree on a time and place for the peace council. On the morning of March 10, Abe paced the veranda of John Fairchild's ranch house. Winema had taken a message to Captain Jack the day before urging him again to come for a peace council, but Jack had resisted. "Still too many soldiers. I think it is a trap. John Fairchild did not send the soldiers away."

"But he did send many of them away. There are only half as many as last week. Come and talk," urged Winema. "You'll be safe."

Actually, General Canby hadn't wanted to send any soldiers away. He felt it would leave the ranch vulnerable if the Modocs chose to attack. It was only with the combined insistence of Abe, Fairchild, and Meacham that he finally agreed to send Batteries A, E, and M of the 4th Artillery on to Van Bremer's ranch. That actually positioned them indirectly between Fairchild's ranch and the Lava Beds and therefore much closer to the Modocs, but it technically did reduce the number at the designated council site.

Winema had come riding in the night before with what she said was the best deal she could make: "Captain Jack said that if he saw another fifty soldiers ride away from the Fairchild ranch in the morning, he would come on in."

"Fifty men!" said Canby. "I'll not do it. Even if he has no plans for an attack, yielding to demands like that is capitulation. That's no way to start negotiating."

"There might be another way to look at it," said Meacham. "You might think you are starting from a position of weakness if you give in to his demand, but that's not necessarily the way these Modocs think. If you do something he asks, then he owes you—he's beholdin' to you. If we are careful, we can call in that favor at an opportune time in the future, maybe at the moment you need to clinch a treaty, for instance."

"Well," said Canby after a time, "as enticing as that is, I'm responsible for the safety of my men, and I feel like I've reduced my strength here as far as I dare."

"Begging your pardon, General," broke in Colonel Mason, "but there's one way we could meet Captain Jack's demand while maintaining our strength."

"How's that, Colonel?"

"If I sent a messenger back to General Gillem at Lost River Ford, he could dispatch fifty men and have them ride over here tonight under cover of darkness. Then at dawn we could send out the fifty men Captain Jack wants to see leaving this place, and we'd not be any weaker."

"Hmm. It might work. But those Indians aren't dumb or blind. They're likely to get wind of us moving that many men, even if it is dark. Still . . ." Canby got up and went over to stare out the window. "I guess it's worth a try. And I'm sure not about to let this place be under-manned."

"Well, we'll just have to pray that it does work," said Reverend Thomas.

Now the appointed day had arrived. The cavalry had ridden out just after dawn, making noise and stirring up as much dust as possible to be sure that any Indians watching the ranch from the surrounding hills could not miss their departure.

Abe had been pacing the porch ever since. He didn't like the trick, and feared Captain Jack wouldn't show. Hours went by.

He had coffee and biscuits and went back to his vigil on the veranda.

Noon had passed when he saw something coming up Tickner Road at the south end of the gentle valley. Could it be? Yes . . . riders. He watched for several more minutes as hope grew. There were five horsemen, and they weren't cavalry. They were either settlers or Indians.

And then Abe was sure. "They're comin' in," yelled Abe. "Captain Jack's on his way."

General Canby came out of the house and Meacham came out of his tent. Soon there was a welcoming delegation waiting for the Indians to ride in. Canby had already given orders to have his remaining troops in position around the ranch and in the army camp. Most were out of sight, but none were out of range to be of help in case of an emergency.

When the Indians arrived, John Fairchild invited them in for some refreshment. The Indian delegation included Captain Jack, Boston Charley, Hooker Jim, and two other Modocs whom Abe didn't know. Scarfaced Charley was not among them, and this worried Abe because Scarfaced Charley was an influential member of the tribe.

Shortly, the Indians, General Canby, Meacham, Reverend Thomas, Abe, John Fairchild, and Winema went over to Meacham's tent. He had a large canvas awning erected for shade. Chairs were brought for the general and Captain Jack. Jack, however, chose to sit on the ground, leaving the chair for Meacham. The council began with formal introductions and assurances of good will.

Finally Captain Jack said, "I come to talk peace. How do you talk, General?"

"That's what we are here for, too. The fighting must stop. Now I know you Modocs have had some trouble with the settlers, and Mr. Meacham, here, has told me how unfairly you were treated when you tried to live with the Klamaths on their reservation. But I think we can work these problems out if we can be sure of ending the fighting."

"Modocs don't want to fight anymore. Killing is bad. All we want is a home on Lost River. We are not Klamaths; we cannot live with those dogs; we'd have to kill them. But we don't want to fight, not even the Klamaths. We just want our own home."

"I'm glad to hear you don't want to fight anymore. We, too, want peace, and I'm sure we can work out everything else."

"Maybe you a good man," said Jack. "We will see."

"I'll tell you what we'll do," said the general. "I represent the United States Army, and Mr. Meacham here speaks for the Great Father in Washington, and the Reverend Thomas—we will make a pact with you, Captain Jack."

"What is pact?"

"A solemn promise. We have the authority of the United States Army and the Great Father in Washington. Anything we promise, we can do for you. We, on our side, promise that we will not commit any treachery or acts of war as long as these peace councils are going so long as you do not commit any treachery or acts of war on your side. Will you agree to that?"

"It's what God wants you to do," put in Thomas.

Captain Jack looked steadily at the general. "Does this 'no treachery' include not sneaking soldiers in after dark to make it look like you send fifty riders away this morning like I asked?"

Canby's face stiffened. "But I did send out the men like you asked," he protested.

"Hmm. Same as you brought in. No change."

Abe's heart clutched, and he saw the general's face go white.

"But that was before I knew you were a good man," pleaded the general. "Until I met you, I didn't know whether I could trust you. So what do you say to our pact? Will you agree to it?"

"I agree." Captain Jack stood up, and the general responded in kind. "General Canby, I want to tell you that my word is good and solid as a big rock. I will live up to my pact with you men as long as you do. You will find this out yourself. But it will surprise me if you live up to your part of the pact, for it will be the first time any white man stands by their word to Modoc Indians. I do really hope from the bottom of my heart, General, that you will keep your promise within reach of your memory from now on."

The general laughed. "I can assure you, Jack, that I meant what I said. You shall see, my strong brave"—he said as he slapped the chief on the back—"that you are entering an agreement with a man."

Then Jack held out his hand to Canby. "General, two men have met. I profess to be a man, too, even if I am nothing but an Indian."

Chapter 21

*T*he next ten days were busy with preparations to move the military headquarters and most of the army to a location within actual sight of Captain Jack's stronghold. The Lava Beds shot one arm north along the west side of Tule Lake. The land to the west of this arm descended gradually for about eight miles to Van Bremer's ranch. But the east side of the arm dropped off abruptly about five hundred feet to the valley below in which was Tule Lake. It was on the foot of this bluff— perhaps a half mile wide, between the bluff and the lakeshore—that the army relocated. "Gillem's Camp" they were calling it because General A.C. Gillem had selected the site. Captain Jack's stronghold was southeast, not more than a mile and a half away, around the bottom of the lake.

Abe didn't like the move, and he knew Meacham didn't either. He'd tried several times to talk with General Canby about it. But it wasn't until the move was actually in progress that Canby paid any attention to him.

"Hey, Miller, come on up here. I need to talk to you." The general dropped out of formation and waited for Abe to ride up. "I have another assignment for you," he said. "I want you to go see Captain Jack again and set up another council. We don't want him to think the talks have stopped. We must keep his hopes up."

"Sir, that's exactly what I've been wanting to talk to you about. Why are you moving your troops so close? Won't this frighten or even infuriate the Indians? And isn't it a violation of the pact you made with Captain Jack?"

"Not at all, young man," the general said as he nudged his bay out of the cloud of dust the column of men were stirring up. "It might scare that renegade a little—which is exactly what I intend to do. But it's not a violation of our pact. It's not an act of war, and it's not treachery. It's a maneuver designed as a show of force."

"How can you move a whole army onto his doorstep and claim it's not an act of war?"

"I'm not moving the whole army down there, only the five hundred men under Gillem's command. We will keep Colonel Mason's men—another four hundred—in reserve, across Tule Lake. Besides, we're not attacking, or shooting anyone. We just want to be ready. But more importantly—in terms of achieving peace—I want Captain Jack to see what he's facing. I want him to know that violent resistance is totally futile."

"You may not be shooting, but it looks pretty aggressive to me."

"Listen, Miller, I don't want to fight those Indians anymore than you do, and that's the truth. But you simply don't understand military matters. In fact, I'm not sure you understand the real world at all." The general slapped his leg and stared south down Tickner Road. "Confound it, boy, why am I even trying to explain this to you?"

The column had arrived at Van Bremer's ranch and was turning east, cross-country toward Tule Lake and Captain Jack's stronghold. Abe caught his breath. It was beautiful country . . . so open, so virgin.

"Look," said Canby, irritably. "I need a messenger, and if I'm going to use you, you need to understand what's happening, or you're liable to say something that gets those poor beggars killed. There's no way under the sun that the United States Government is going to allow a small band of renegades—with fifty-some braves—to run around the country threatening and killing settlers."

Abe started to protest, but Canby held up his hand. "Now

I'm not defending everything those settlers have done. I'm sure some of them provoked the attacks. But this country is changing, and the notion of just letting those Indians run free and set up camp when and where they please is never going to happen again. That's a thing of the past.

"I have my orders. They came straight from Washington: 'Go to Lost River and move Captain Jack and his band of Modoc Indians onto the Klamath reservation, peaceably if you can, but forcibly if you must.' Now that's going to happen, Mr. Miller, as certain as the sun rises in the east. It . . . will . . . happen! So you tell me—since you're so interested in avoiding bloodshed—what's the worst thing that could occur?"

"Well," Abe stumbled, "I guess if the army went in and wiped them all out."

"I'm not going to do that as long as we're talking. Think again."

Abe's head was spinning. Canby had orders to move the Modocs onto the Klamath reservation? No negotiating room whatsoever? "Maybe Captain Jack not getting the home he wants on Lost River."

"Well, that's Meacham's department. I don't make policy. I'd like to see the Indians get their home back, too. But let me tell you, the very worst thing that could happen right now would be for Captain Jack to get the idea that he can win anything by fighting. And that's why I'm moving my troops to this new location. I want Captain Jack to see me daily. I want every one of his braves, his squaws, his children, to see us. They have to know what they're up against. They must realize that fighting won't get them anywhere. Accepting that could save their lives. It's only fair to them."

Abe turned in his saddle. "Fair? You think bullying them like that is fair, sir? There's no justice in that. The just thing is to grant them what they want—what's theirs. Is it so much to ask—a small reservation in their homeland?"

"The just thing?" General Canby snorted. "The only real

justice for the Indian would be to expel the white man entirely from this continent. That's the only way the Indians could return to their old way of life. But you and I both know that's not going to happen. Call it man's greed or the tides of human history or whatever you want. It's not going to happen. Only God can dispense true justice. You should know that, Mr. Miller—you're a religious man. And if you go around encouraging those Indians to hold out for 'justice,' they'll sure enough try . . . and die. And their blood will be on your hands."

General Canby kicked his horse into an easy canter and regained the front of the column. Abe followed and reined in beside Canby once more.

"How can you say that?" Abe protested. "I'm not the one who's trying to take their land. I'm not the one representing a government that keeps breaking its treaties with them. I'm not prepared to smash them with an army twenty times their size. How can you say their blood would be on my hands?"

"Because in refusing to face reality, you're feeding their lethal fantasies! You can't change the course of history, Mr. Miller. And you can't dispense justice. The most you can hope to do is avoid doing evil yourself, and maybe, just maybe, if you're lucky, you'll get the chance to prevent a few people's deaths. If you can accomplish that, you will have made a positive contribution to peace."

Abe shook his head in frustration. "But that doesn't deal with the roots of injustice."

"If that's what you want to do, you better become a preacher, because it's inside each person that that battle is won or lost."

"I don't understand. Somebody has to fight for the rights of those Indians—and I don't mean with guns."

"You don't intend it to be with guns, but once certain things are set in motion, you don't know what will happen. That's why I'm concerned that you take care what you say to those

Modocs. They mustn't entertain fantasies about what they can accomplish by resisting."

"So that gives you the right to threaten violence as the way to make 'em do what the white man wants?"

"Face it, Miller. The 'sword' of the U.S. Government is currently in power. And it's not likely to be displaced in the immediate future. In that sense, and maybe that sense only, it's ordained by God. To resist it is folly. My job is to move those Indians to a reservation. I want to do it in a way that saves as many lives as possible. The Indian has a long, hard road ahead of him. He cannot continue in his old way of life. For that reason, the reservation may be a slow death too, but it does buy him time to come into the modern world . . . if he will."

They had been riding up a long and gentle rise, and now they paused on the crest of a bluff overlooking Tule Lake. A bluish haze hung in the shadows of the valley below. A little to their right tents already checkered the bivouac area along the lake's shore. Horses milled in a circular stone corral. A large tent with a flag and the units' guidons indicated headquarters. Together, Abe and the general nudged their horses down the steep trail ahead of the long column of troops. As they left the comfort of the afternoon sun, chilly breezes rose to meet them.

Abe had one more question while he had the general's attention. "What about people like Reno Bauder who use the government—who use you and your army—to grab land that rightfully belongs to the Modocs? Don't you have any qualms about being his henchman?"

Canby grimaced. "Bauder's part of the tide that's hard to stop or even control. I know he hates the Modocs, and he's been a real pain in the neck to me, but so far, I'm not aware that he's done anything illegal."

"Didn't Meacham tell you?"

"Tell me what?"

But before Abe had a chance to explain, several men came

out of the headquarters tent to meet the general. In their midst strode Reno Bauder.

"Well, General," Bauder bellowed. "Now we're getting down to business. By the way, I brought you a little gift this morning. Check out the corral over there . . . twenty-three of the finest Indian ponies you'll ever find."

"Where'd you get 'em?" asked Canby, frowning.

"Me and the boys found 'em straying off toward the lake as we rode over here this morning. 'Course there were a couple Indian brats tagging along after 'em. But they couldn't keep up, so I took 'em to be a herd of wild horses and rounded them up for you."

"General, you can't keep those horses!" Abe said. "They're Captain Jack's, and that would be a violation of your pact for sure."

"Well, well, if it isn't that Yellowbelly Miller," growled Bauder. "Sticking your nose where it doesn't belong again, I see. What are you doing down here again, anyway?"

"He's been serving as an envoy to Captain Jack for me," said General Canby. "Seems the chief trusts him."

"I wouldn't doubt it," said Bauder.

Abe ignored the big rancher. "General . . . what about those ponies?"

"Don't worry about it, Miller. We'll get 'em back to 'em sometime . . . maybe they'll make a good bargaining chip. Go set up your tent and report to me this evening after chow," said the general abruptly. Dismounting, he ducked into the command tent.

• • •

When Abe and Winema visited the Modocs to set up a second peace council, the Indians' response was just as Abe expected.

"I know those soldiers intend to kill me and all my people," said Captain Jack. "If they did not, why have they moved in on us with so many men?"

"There's not going to be any killing as long as the peace talks proceed," said Abe.

"How can I believe the white man when he steals my horses? I want my horses back."

"Talk to the general. I'm sure you will get them back."

It took Abe and Winema most of a day to get them to agree to another peace council. Captain Jack finally said, "I am a true Modoc. I am not afraid to die. I am not afraid of them brass buttons. Tell the Commissioners, I will meet with them in council tomorrow."

But then, the issue was where to meet. They flatly refused to come to the army camp for the meeting. In the end, Abe persuaded them to meet halfway between their stronghold and Gillem's Camp.

The army erected a tent in the flat field. Only occasional juniper trees and huge stones tossed there by some prehistoric eruption broke up the low sage brush and thin bunch grass. It was a good spot. There was not enough cover for anyone to stage an ambush. And anyone approaching the site could be seen from far away for plenty of warning. The site was also easily observable by field glasses from Gillem's Camp to the northwest and by the Modocs to the southeast. Some of them even climbed to the top of rocks in their stronghold to watch the proceedings.

Captain Jack, Scarfaced Charley, and a sub-chief named John Schonchin (whom Abe had never talked to) were already at the council site on the morning of March 27 when the government's contingent consisting of General Canby, Reverend Thomas, Alfred Meacham, Abe Miller, and Winema Riddle arrived.

The Indians did not want to enter the tent, so everyone sat in a circle on the ground in front.

Captain Jack opened the council by saying, "General, we

make peace quick if you meet me halfway. It takes two to agree on anything. You, General, want to lay plan and want me to agree with you, which I cannot do. But if you will agree to even half of what I and my people want, we get along fine."

At that the general sat up straight and stroked his clean-shaven chin. "Now you listen to me, Captain Jack. This is no way to reach peace. You do not dictate to me. My job is to make peace with you . . . nothing else."

"But General, you not dictate to me, either. I'm not your prisoner or slave—not today anyway. All I ask of you is a reservation along Lost River, or near the Fairchild's ranch."

"You know I cannot do that, Jack."

"Then give me Lava Beds for our home. No white man ever want to make homes here."

Meacham spoke up. "Jack, neither the general nor any of us can promise you a place until you agree that all fighting and killing will stop."

"If that is the way you explain it to me," said Jack, "then how we ever make peace? I will not agree on anything you men ask until you agree to give me a home in my native country."

Canby frowned. "Captain Jack, you never could live here and get along with the white people in this country because there has been blood spilt here by your people."

"If that true," answered Captain Jack, "we can never make peace or be safe in any country."

"Listen to me," said General Canby. "You Indians have to come under the white man's laws. The white man's law is strong and straight and will treat you justly."

"All I want is promise that you will give us a home in this country."

"But we cannot make you that promise. It would never work," Reverend Thomas echoed.

General Canby was getting exasperated with the direction of the conversation. "Jack, all you have to do is get your people together and come out under a flag of truce. A white flag means peace. No one will hurt you under a white flag."

The Modoc Indians looked at each other.

"I know about white flags," said Captain Jack. "Let me tell you true story, General. When I was a boy, a white man named Ben Wright called forty-five of my people to come to a peace feast under flag of truce. Several settlers also came . . . Reno Bauder was one of them. How many Modocs do you think got away with their lives?"

Captain Jack leaned forward and held up his right hand with five fingers extended. Staring intently into the general's eyes, he slowly closed his thumb and first two fingers. "Two of them still live today," he said, jerking his head back toward the Lava Beds. "They will not let my people forget what a white flag means. I could never get them to come out under so-called flag of truce."

The general squirmed. "Well . . . that was wrong, of course."

"Was it?" asked Jack. "Then why did white people in Yreka give Ben Wright a big dinner and dance that night and call him hero? Why didn't he have to face white man's law?"

Reverend Thomas intervened. "Jack, that was a long time ago. We're different men. We are not like Ben Wright. We want to help you and your people live in peace."

"If you want to help us, give me and my people a home here in our own country. We will harm no one if we are left alone."

"Look," said Canby, "don't keep asking us for something that is not in our power to grant. I've told you and John Schonchin that we are unable to give or even promise you a home in this country."

"My true man," said Captain Jack, "do you remember pact we made at Fairchild's ranch not many days ago? At that council, you told me that any terms you reached with me, the Great Father in Washington would do. Now you tell me you have no power to do for me what I ask. Which is it?"

Anger flushed Canby's face. Abe looked anxiously at Meacham. Why wasn't the man saying anything? Someone had to ease things between Jack and the general.

On impulse, Abe extended his hand in a calming gesture. "Captain Jack," he said urgently, "let me be the next to talk. We want to make peace with you, and we are going to do it. We all have to trust God, who wants all men to be brothers! If we agree to peace, everything will come around right."

Jack smiled faintly. "Crazy Abe, I may trust God . . . but I cannot trust these men who wear blue cloth and brass buttons."

This made the general all the more angry. "What has this blue cloth and brass buttons done to you?" he challenged.

"The soldiers shot our women and babies!" Captain Jack growled through clenched teeth.

"Didn't your braves kill innocent settlers too?"

"Not women and children . . . and I wasn't part of raids on settlers. The only men we shot weren't innocent. Soldiers were the first to fire on my people on north banks along Lost River. And you know that, General."

Abe intervened again. "Please, Captain Jack, let's not get angry. We cannot make peace this way. You too, General Canby. Let's hold our tempers. There's too much at stake to let peace slip away."

"You're right, Miller," said Canby, mopping his brow with a handkerchief. "Let's proceed more calmly, okay, Jack?"

"Okay, General. But . . . you say we cannot have home in our own country because we killed settlers, right?"

"That's right. You see, Captain Jack, the settlers would never treat you right . . . unless you gave up those men who murdered the settlers. Then we might arrange for you to live in this country."

Captain Jack raised his eyebrows. "Now we get somewhere, General. Will you give me your men who shot our women and children?"

"Come on, Jack," the general laughed. "Only one law can live at a time, and your people have no law."

The Indian chief took the insult quietly for a few moments,

then said, "This is what I'll do, Canby. If you will give up your men who shot our women and children to be tried by your law, I'll give up Modocs who shot settlers to be tried by same law."

Canby looked uncomfortable. "Uh, I can't do that, Jack. Our men who killed your squaws and children did it in war."

Jack's eyes narrowed. "So did we. It is time of war, is it not? That's why we have to have peace council."

Meacham interrupted. "We're not getting very far. I think we'd better quit for the day. Maybe in our next council we can come to terms."

"I have my doubts," spoke up Scarfaced Charley for the first time. "If peace talkers don't have power to do anything for Modocs, what good is talking? But we reach some agreement—that for sure. So many soldiers camped here are not here for any good . . . I know it. I feel it. I see it."

"Don't be afraid," assured Abe. "The soldiers won't hurt you while we're talking peace."

"I didn't say I was afraid, Crazy Abe."

General Canby stood up. "When you're ready, Captain Jack, let us know, and we'll have our next council meeting."

Abe watched as the three Indians mounted their ponies and rode away. Why was Meacham leaving all the talking to Canby? Wasn't Meacham the head of this Peace Commission? Maybe Canby meant well, but he was a military man; his bottom line was following orders, and he had the firepower to back them up.

At least the two sides were still talking . . . so why did he feel a sick foreboding in his stomach?

Chapter 22

*A*be's frustration with the peace councils and disappointment with Meacham gnawed at him constantly. Several days after the second council, he decided to visit the Modocs. The prospects for peace seemed to be slipping fast. Captain Jack was insistent on a reservation along Lost River, but General Canby was unwilling to make any promises. It was a standoff. Still, Abe believed that a reservation of their own for the Modocs was reasonable. If only they could be patient and persistent, certainly "right" would ultimately prevail.

He went alone to the Modoc stronghold, without Winema and Fairchild, and although no one came out to escort him, he was sure he had been watched. He arrived at the open area around which the tribe camped as some kind of council was in progress. John Schonchin and Hooker Jim were addressing the assembled tribe, but Captain Jack was nowhere to be seen.

No one welcomed Abe or seemed to notice his presence, so he sat at the edge of the firelight and tried to figure out what was going on. However, since the Indians were speaking Modoc and Winema was not there to translate, Abe could decipher very little. The speeches went on and on, sometimes in very heated fashion. It was obvious to Abe that they were talking about their situation. Frequent gestures indicated the army camp, their own stronghold, and acts of fighting. But what they were actually saying escaped him.

Finally the discussion stopped, and a squaw was sent away. In a few minutes she returned with Captain Jack. He looked at Abe but said nothing to him.

Schonchin then embarked on a long speech to Captain Jack. And why he did it, Abe didn't know, but Schonchin began dropping in enough English words and phrases so that— along with his tone and gestures—Abe began to get the drift of the discourse. Apparently, the Indians wanted to give up the peace process. When Schonchin made a point, the rest of the tribe hooted and shouted agreement.

Jack repeatedly shook his head and waved his hand discounting the harangues until Hooker Jim stepped up and yelled in his face, his nose not four inches from Jack's. Then Hooker Jim jammed a squaw's hat on Jack's head and threw a shawl over his shoulders. Jack stood stoically, staring ahead as though he were facing the wind alone on the top of a mountain. Then someone tripped him and threw him down on his back. Another spat on him.

Abe couldn't believe the tribe was treating its war chief so contemptuously. How could they get away with it?

Jack scrambled to his feet, threw off the hat and shawl, and yelled angrily back to them, then stalked off to his cave. The others began dancing. It looked like a war dance with sham battles and wild yells.

Abe inched his way farther back into the shadows. Should he stand and address the tribe or get out of there while he could? Things looked bad. But still no one paid any attention to him, so finally he decided to find a place to sleep and try to talk to Captain Jack in the morning when things had cooled off. Jack still seemed his best hope.

In the morning, he found Captain Jack's cave and slipped in. The Indian looked up, then yelled and threw a bone at his wives and children. They scurried out. Abe sat down and remained silent for several minutes. At last he ventured, "What'd that mean last night? Are you still the chief?"

"Yes . . . but only war chief. Dead chief of a dead tribe."

"What do you mean? There's still hope for a peaceful settlement."

Captain Jack turned his head and stared over Abe's shoulder. "Modocs know soldiers here to kill them."

"No . . . no! The peace councils are still happening. We can schedule a third one. Prospects are good."

Jack turned back and glared at Abe. "Then why do more and more soldiers arrive every two, three days? Why point those big guns at us? They shoot bullets as big as your head."

"But they won't use them as long as we're talking peace."

"Only fog stopped them from shooting our heads off with those big guns in the last battle. Hooker Jim say strong medicine stop big guns," Jack scoffed, "but I know it was just fog. But maybe . . . who knows?" He gazed out of the cave's opening. "Maybe fog come from strong medicine . . . But I think Modoc medicine run out. I think Modocs are dead."

"That's not true, Captain Jack," Abe said desperately. "You are a strong man, a strong chief. You can use that strength to win your cause with General Canby. Your strength is the strength of ten because your cause is just."

His mind scrambled. "Let me tell you a story, a story from God's Book," he continued. "Once there was an evil tribe who besieged God's people much as the blue coats have besieged you. They were far more powerful than God's people, and they had a great giant who came out each day and taunted God's people.

"But God told a young boy to take his sling and five smooth stones and go out and meet the giant. When he did, the giant laughed at him, but the boy flung the stone and hit the giant right between the eyes and killed him. And God's people were free."

Abe leaned forward intensely. "Jack, you're like that young boy. The cause of your people is just. And the stone with which you can defeat the giant bluecoats is your persistence. There are a lot of newspaper men around here. Some of them are sympathetic to your cause. When the people of this country read what they write, they will realize how unjustly you are being treated. Then they will force the politicians to grant you a reservation on Lost River. You've got to have faith, Jack, faith that you can win."

Jack shook his head slowly. "I don't know. Who cares about Indians? Who cares about Modocs?"

"Lots of people, Jack. But we've got to give them time to hear about your situation so they can come together to back you. Good people everywhere will unite for the Modocs. You'll see; there are other ways to win than with guns. For instance, you know what we need to do? We need to get some newspaper man to tell about how the army killed your women and children on Lost River. That'll wake people up. It really shocked me when you told that story the other day."

"Modocs never kill women and children. Bluecoats should pay."

"I understand how you feel. Being a white man myself, I feel terrible; I feel responsible for what they did. And other white people—the just ones—will feel the same, and they'll want to give you what you deserve. You have the right to a home of your own on Lost River."

"What you mean, Crazy Abe? Why you feel responsible? You weren't there."

"But it's my people who are treating the Indians so badly. However, if we can publicize that incident, it will show the world the injustice you are experiencing, and maybe we can force a change."

"Yes. We make change happen. I think bluecoats pay."

"Maybe they will. But the most important thing you need to do is not give up. Remember your five smooth stones, and you can take out the giant. When there's justice, then there'll be peace."

"Maybe you not so Crazy Abe. No justice, no peace. That sound good. No peace without justice."

They agreed that the next peace council would happen on April 11, and Abe left the stronghold greatly encouraged. If anyone could help the Modocs hold a steady course, it was Captain Jack. When he reported to Canby that Captain Jack was open to another peace council, the general seemed hopeful too.

Since the next meeting was several days off, Abe decided to ride up to Linkville, get a bath, some hot meals . . . and maybe see Mary again.

• • •

All the way to Linkville, Abe thought about the last time he had seen Mary, and the delightful tingle of his lips against hers. He couldn't wait to see her again and share his good news. Prospects for peace between the army and the Modocs were looking up. Maybe soon life would return to normal in the region.

He had wanted to speak of marriage to Mary the last time they had been together, but she had brushed him off as though she didn't want to face the question. He could understand. With so much violence between the Indians and the settlers, and so much tension between him and her father, talk of marriage might have been premature. Maybe now, with higher hopes for peace, she would listen to him. He was sure she cared for him. She hadn't objected to his kiss, and a woman like Mary wouldn't allow that unless she was open.

He stopped by the bank to see if Mary was working, but the bank was closed, so he went to George Nurse's hotel for a room, but there was none to be had. "Well, is Jonathan Davis staying here?" Abe asked.

"Yeah, he still has a room rented," said George, "but he's away for a couple days. I think he said he was goin' to talk to some scab-rock farmers west of here about putting up fencing or something."

"Yeah, that's Davis. We're good friends," said Abe. "I'll stay in his room."

"I don't know about that," said the hotel keeper. "What if he comes back tonight and wants a place to sleep?"

"Hey, don't you remember? He let me stay in his room last December. We're almost partners."

"Oh, yeah. You're the guy who went into the Modoc camp." That was enough to persuade George Nurse, and so Abe got a room, took a bath, and then went over to the Widow Morgan's place, guessing that Mary would be staying there again. The surprise on Mary's face when she answered the door transformed to a quick smile of joy as she said, "Abe! Come in. I'm so glad to see you."

"Before I track up the floor, I was wondering if I'm too late to take you over to Nurse's for some dinner."

"Well, I don't know. I'll need to speak to Mrs. Morgan. I'd invite you to eat here, but she's not feeling too well tonight."

"I wouldn't think of imposing myself."

Mary was back in a minute with her coat and hat, and they headed out into the crisp April evening.

During their meal, Abe didn't notice that the steak was tough, the beans were too salty, and the crust on the apple pie was as stiff as mule skin. All he cared about was watching Mary's bright eyes as she told about her job at the bank and her new friendship with some women in town. "And," she said, wiping her mouth with her napkin, "I've been helping some at the school. I don't think Mrs. Thatcher has had more than a sixth grade education. She reads everything she can get her hands on, but the poor kids still need more."

"Mary," ventured Abe, leaning over the little table with its calico cloth, "do you remember the last time we were together?"

"Sure . . . out at the ranch. I was so busy that day."

"Well, I was wondering . . . I mean, things with the Modocs are improving. We're going to get a peace settlement any day now. And then things around here will calm down, don't you think?"

"I'm sure of it. As terrible as this war has been, it's made

Linkville boom, what with all the freight coming through and all. And Lord knows, there're always soldiers in town. I'm surprised you found a room."

"I took Jonathan Davis's room. He's out for a couple days."

Several teamsters came into the small cafe just then, stamping the mud off their feet. Abe watched as they looked around for a table—there were only three other tables in the place, all close to Mary and Abe. "Mary, maybe we could go for a walk . . . if it isn't too cold for you," Abe said, rising from his chair.

"No. I'll be fine."

Outside, they walked in silence past Manning's livery barn toward the lake. Mary took Abe's arm as he guided her around the muddy spots created by the many horses and wagons. The moon reflected off Klamath Lake, and they walked out on the planks of the makeshift pier as though they were stepping on the moonbeams in the water.

With a deep sigh, Mary said, "It's beautiful, isn't it?"

"Yes . . . though not half so beautiful as you are. Listen, Mary," he said as he gently turned her toward him. "I was thinkin' . . . when this thing is all over—with the Modocs and all—would you be willing to marry me?"

Mary's eyes flew wider, startled. Then: "Oh, Abe," she sighed and laid her head against his chest.

He waited, trying to keep the excitement he felt from causing his whole body to tremble.

Finally she said, "Abe, I do think that I love you, but . . . well, this whole war thing is very confusing—"

"But it's gonna be over soon."

"I hope so. But there's something about . . . about the way you've gotten involved in this whole thing. You worry me, Abe, thinking you know how to stop the war, when . . . when bigger men than you realize how complicated it all is."

"But shouldn't we all work for peace, Mary? I know you don't want this war anymore than I do."

"I know, Abe, but . . ." Suddenly, she reached up and kissed him.

Abe slid his hands around her and pulled her tight. The soft curves of her body pressed against him, and he drew out the kiss as long as he could.

When Mary broke free, she was breathless. With her hands on his chest, she pushed him back a little and said, "Abe . . . let that . . . let that be enough on the subject for now. Okay?"

"Sure, Mary, but—"

"Just walk me home for now, Abe. Just walk me home."

They walked in silence, Abe wondering what was going on in her mind and wishing he hadn't promised General Canby that he would return to camp the next morning. If he only had a little more time with her . . .

On the steps of the Widow Morgan's, Mary gave Abe a quick peck on the cheek, and simply said, "Good night, Abe Miller. I want you to know that I—I pray for you every night." Then she was gone.

Chapter 23

When Abe returned to camp on April 10, an orderly ran up to him as soon as he rode in to say that the general was expecting him immediately for a meeting in his tent.

Already assembled were Meacham, John Fairchild, Winema, and Leroy Dyar, the Klamath reservation agent. They were all sitting around a table that General Canby headed. Abe took a seat and soon Reverend Thomas also arrived.

"I want to make plans for the council tomorrow," Canby began. "Meacham, here, has some hopeful information."

"Yes. I've been working hard on arrangements for the Modocs. Dyar has agreed to submit a report recommending that the Modocs not be returned to the Klamath reservation. Apparently, their claims of mistreatment by the far more numerous Klamaths are well founded. They frequently did not receive the blankets and supplies that the government promised them."

"But I don't see how we can grant them a place on the Lost River," said Canby. "With the way Bauder and some other settlers feel, there'd never be peace."

"Not even if Captain Jack were willing to surrender those that did the killing of the settlers?" asked Dyar.

"That's not really the issue," said Meacham. "It's land—land pure and simple. That section along Lost River is the best grazing for miles around, and the settlers'll keep after it until they get it."

"Then what are we going to do?" said Canby.

Abe spoke up. "I don't see how you can just allow a greedy

land grabber to get away with taking what rightfully belongs to the Indians."

"That's not the point," said Meacham. "Through Washington, I could probably force a decision to get them that reservation, but that wouldn't be the end of it. Without peace with their neighbors, there'd continue to be 'incidents,' and sooner or later they would lead to serious trouble—maybe another uprising and a lot of bloodshed. But there is one other option that I've been working on . . ."

"Go ahead," urged Canby.

"Well, it's a place about fifty miles south of here . . . as the crow flies, that is. Big Valley, they call it. You probably know it, Fairchild. The town of Adin sits in the northeast corner of the valley. Anyway, it's a beautiful valley, and I'm trying to get the Modocs a place there."

"What do you think, Winema?" asked Canby. "Do you think Captain Jack would agree to that?"

"Maybe."

"But won't the people down there be aware of the Modocs?" asked Abe.

"And what about the Pit River Indians?" said Fairchild. "That's their territory."

"I think the Modocs could live easier with the Pits than the Klamaths. The Klamaths are their longtime enemies. I never realized that when we stuck them on the reservation before. I thought that because they spoke the same language, they would get along. But they've been feuding for generations. Now, as for the whites in Big Valley, I'm sure they are up-to-date on all that's been happening, but there isn't the bad blood like there has been around here. It'll take some convincing, but I think we can do it."

"I hope so," said General Canby. "We need to clinch this thing tomorrow. I don't know how much longer we can drag out these peace councils."

At that moment there was a great commotion outside the

tent. Abe recognized Bauder's booming voice: "Let me pass. I've got to see the general. It's urgent! I must talk to him right now."

Suddenly he burst through the tent flap. "General Canby, you've got to call off this peace council."

"How come? What's the problem?"

"I just found out that they plan to kill you—every one of you Peace Commissioners."

"What do you mean? How do you know?"

"There's a Modoc that used to work for me once in a while, roundin' up cattle and so forth. He's one of the few Modocs that's worth his salt. Name's Weium. And when I was ridin' in from Hospital Rock this morning, he jumps out from behind a juniper, spooked my horse somethin' fierce. I almost shot that cursed savage, but he kept holdin' up his hands and puttin' his finger to his mouth to hush me. If it had been anyone else, I guess I would have shot him.

"Anyway, he told me that Captain Jack, Hooker Jim, John Schonchin, and some of the others are planning to kill you tomorrow."

"That can't be!" said Abe angrily. "Captain Jack would never do that. I just talked to him the other day."

"Shut up, Miller," shouted Bauder. "I know all about you talking to him. Weium told me you were in their camp, but you don't know what you're doin'. It's true," he said, turning back to the general, "that Jack didn't want to kill anyone, but several of the other braves are fed up with the delays. They forced Captain Jack to agree to shoot you, General."

"How could they do that? He's the chief," said Canby.

"He's only a sub-chief, a war chief. If he doesn't shoot you, they will kill him. It's that simple. They don't trust Jack any longer," explained Bauder.

"Are you sure about this, Bauder?" asked Canby, frowning.

"Of course I'm sure, and I believe Weium too."

Abe jumped to his feet. "You're just trying to sabotage these peace talks. All you've wanted from the beginning is to wipe out the Modocs, and now that peace is within our reach, you—you . . ."

"Hold on there, Miller," cautioned the general. "We need to pay attention to this. It could be a warning that we dare not disregard. Tell us more, Bauder. Were there any other details?"

"Weium said that the night Miller was in camp several of the braves threatened Captain Jack. Said that if Jack wouldn't agree to kill you, General, they'd kill him, right then and there. They kept calling him a coward and an old squaw. They even knocked him down and spat on him. This really upset Weium, 'cause I guess he's pretty loyal.

"And Miller, if you had any brains in your head, you'd've figured out what was going on and reported it," Bauder spat. "Anyway, according to Weium, Captain Jack finally agreed, and they left him alone. The next day he asked the whole tribe to release him from his promise. He was sure there was still hope for peace."

"That's right," said Abe. "I did a lot to encourage him, to help him believe that he could win."

"You encouraged him that he could do what?" demanded Canby with a horrified look on his face.

"That he could . . . that his cause was just, that if he would persist, the Modocs could get a home for themselves. You know . . . just like Meacham was saying a little while ago. It's possible. It's more than possible! It's gonna happen if we . . . if we don't withdraw the olive branch."

"Yeah, well they're fixin' to persist, all right," interrupted Bauder. "They got some plan called 'five smooth stones' or something, and they're gonna assassinate you, General. You and Meacham and the rest."

"No, no they're not," said Abe with relief. "There's nothing to worry about. The 'five smooth stones' was an idea that I gave Jack. I was telling him how he was like young David in the Bible and that he could defeat the giants that are besieging his people, if only he would—"

"'D-defeat the giants'?" stammered Canby. "Is that what you told those savages, Mr. Miller? I warned you about saying anything that would give them hope concerning the path of resistance! I think we'd better heed Bauder's warning, gentlemen. Tomorrow's council is off."

"No!" Abe jumped up, knocking over his chair. "We can't let this chance slip away," he pleaded. "If we don't keep the appointment, the Indians will lose heart. They'll conclude that we don't really want peace. Don't you see? That's just what Bauder wants. Tell 'em, Mr. Meacham. Tell 'em what Bauder's been doin'."

Meacham's eyes squinted, and his head shook ever so slightly.

"Then I'll tell 'em!" blurted Abe, his face flushing red and his eyes going wide. He was through waiting for Meacham to act. "Bauder here has done everything in his power to start this war to wipe out the Modocs. He wants their land for his own ranch on Lost River. He went all the way back to Washington, D.C. and blackmailed the top Indian agent, a man named Kramer. Kramer's married to a society woman in Washington, but he also has an Indian squaw from when he lived here in Oregon. Bauder threatened to tell people in Washington about Kramer's Oregon squaw if Kramer didn't replace Meacham with Odeneal. Kramer buckled and did as he was told. And since then, it's been Odeneal's harsh actions that started the fighting."

"You sniveling cur. I'll teach you to spread lies about me." Bauder stepped toward Abe.

"Take it easy, Mr. Bauder." General Canby stood up between the two men with his hands held out to calm Bauder. "Now tell us, son," he said turning back to Abe, "where did you get this wild story?"

"I heard Bauder speak of it himself, on the train when he was coming back from Washington. You tell 'em, Mr.

Meacham. Isn't it true?"

Everyone turned to Meacham. "I'm afraid it is true. When I was in Washington, I checked it out myself."

There was a moment of silence. Then the general said, "Looks like this changes things. I think we'd better go ahead with the peace council."

"You're fools! You're all fools," snarled Bauder. "What proof do have you?" he challenged Meacham. "What proof is there for this fanciful tale?"

"Well, I don't have any proof yet, Mr. Bauder . . . unless it would be this story you just brought us today trying to sabotage our peace efforts. If your story's a fabrication, then it would strongly indicate that you are prepared to do anything to wipe out those Indians."

"Well, it ain't no lie, and if you don't believe me, it'll be your scalps they'll be liftin', not mine." And Bauder stormed out of the tent.

Chapter 24

*G*eneral Canby was up early Friday morning. In preparation for the next peace council, he assembled Alfred Meacham, Leroy Dyar (the agent of the Klamath reservation), Winema, and Abe.

To the side stood Reverend Elesar Thomas. "General, I think that I should accompany you as well today. I'm sure God's presence will be important . . . to offer a prayer and remind the savages of God's will for them. Besides, I am an official member of this Peace Commission."

"I'd rather you stick with praying for the troops today, Reverend. We don't need you out there for God to be present. As I recall from my catechism, God is present everywhere. And as for prayin'. . ." the general looked around, "we got Miller, here. He's a Mennonite. That ought to do. Besides," the general straightened and drew a deep breath through his nose as his nostrils flared, "I'm not so unfamiliar with speaking to the Almighty, myself. In fact, you can be sure that I've already done a heap of praying this morning, probably before you ever got up."

The general let out a long breath. "The fact is," he confided, "I'd rather our numbers were less today."

"In that case," said Winema, coming forward, "I don't need to go. In fact, I really don't want to attend this council."

"But you're Modoc, woman. We need you, not merely to interpret—Captain Jack speaks good enough English—but we need your presence. It strengthens our hand for the Indians to know that you trust us."

"But I've got a bad feeling about today. I really don't want to go."

"Everyone's got the jitters," said Abe. "But that's because this council is so important."

"Then can Frank come, too?"

The general was exasperated. "Oh, all right. Your husband can come."

"What about me, then?" asked Reverend Thomas.

"All right, you too—but no one else. We can't turn this into a circus . . . Now, I've sent a detail out to set the tent up again. We'll be meeting in the same place as last time, halfway between our camp and the Modoc stronghold. It's in plain sight of everyone. That should put an end to these rumors of treachery. The Modocs would not dare to do anything when they are no more than a half mile from a thousand soldiers."

"General," interjected Meacham in a sad voice, "While I suspect Bauder's motives, maybe we should maintain extra vigilance. Don't forget that these Indians experienced treachery at the hands of white men when Ben Wright and his cohorts murdered them—women and children included—at a peace council."

"Yeah, yeah. I remember all that, but that was a long time ago. I don't think Jack holds any intentions of retaliating. He didn't sound like it the other day."

"He may not, but it set an example of what even white people consider 'honorable' behavior in war. The 'good' people of Yreka turned out to cheer Wright and his men when they returned carrying their bloody trophies of Modoc scalps."

"You can't mean that, Meacham. Surely, civilized people wouldn't condone that kind of behavior today."

"Well, who knows what civilized means today, General. Even our school children go around saying, 'All is fair in love and war.' It might be wise to carry some means of personal protection, maybe a concealed derringer or something."

"Do as you please, but listen to me, every one of you. If anyone sabotages these peace proceedings by displaying a weapon or speaking of it, I will personally see that that person is prosecuted. Furthermore—and this applies especially to you, Miller, since you have taken it onto yourself to disobey me once already—only Meacham, Mr. Dyar, and I have authority to negotiate any specifics of a treaty with the Modocs. Is that understood?"

"Yes, sir," said Abe. Others murmured their assent as well.

"All right then. Be ready to leave in a half hour."

As they left the general's tent, Meacham turned to Abe. "While I don't put much stock in what Bauder said, I'm inclined to trust the misgivings of Winema. She's real nervous. I think I'll write a farewell letter to my wife, just in case."

"Surely you won't need that, Mr. Meacham. We're gonna make peace today, I can feel it in my bones."

"I hope you're right."

Reverend Thomas walked with General Canby out to the council tent ahead of the rest. When Abe and the others arrived a few minutes later, the members of the Indian delegation were all smoking cigars that the general had handed out, and everyone was laughing and talking. Abe sighed in relief. The mood was positive.

"Let's go in the tent and get down to business," said the general.

"We like the fresh air," said Captain Jack. "Let's sit outside to talk."

The general shrugged and smiled. "Whatever you wish. After all, you're the captain, at least for today, right?"

The Modocs present were Captain Jack, John Schonchin, Black Jim, Hooker Jim, Boston Charley, Bogus Charley, and Slolux. Everyone sat down except Abe and Slolux. When Abe saw that Slolux did not sit and that everyone else had more or less teamed up across from one another, he decided to remain standing, too.

Canby opened the meeting by saying, "My Modoc friends,

my heart feels good today. I feel good because you are my friends, and I know we'll do good work today. I know I'll make you see things right today. You will see as I see.

"Jack, I know you are a smart man. That is why I want you to make peace. It's bad to fight. Be a man and live like one. As long as you live in these rocks you won't be living like a man.

"I need to tell you, Jack, that the Great Father in Washington has said that he will not let you live in the Lava Beds. You have been in trouble with his children along the Lost River. He will have to find you a new home far away where there won't be anymore trouble. And it will be a good home. Now how about it? Are you ready to make peace?"

Everyone sat in silence until Captain Jack finally said, "General Canby, your word is as crooked as this," and he held up a twig of sagebrush. "Less than one month ago you promised not to commit any act of war on your side if I would not while we had these peace councils. And I haven't committed any acts of war, have I?"

"No."

"But you, General Canby, moved all your soldiers right over here by my home. You stole and have kept a herd of my ponies. You brought in big guns that shoot balls as big as your head. Aren't all those acts of war?"

"Well, not really. They haven't hurt anyone. Besides—"

"You know very well that they are acts of war, and if you have broken your word to me once, how can I believe you now?"

The general got huffy. "Listen to me, Jack. I did not start this mess, but if you won't make peace, the Great Father has ordered me to use many, many soldiers to come into the Lava Beds and get you and your people and make you come out. And even if you could kill all these soldiers, more would come. What I say is law."

"We cannot make peace with so many soldiers crowding me," said Captain Jack. "Move them back, then we'll talk some more." Jack then looked around at the other Modocs and then waved his hand as though to dismiss his demand. "I'll tell you what, General Canby, now's your chance. Promise me a home somewhere in this country. If it can't be on Lost River, how about over near Hot Creek? Promise me today! Though your word is not much good, I am willing to take your promise. Mr. Meacham will make it strong."

"I cannot do that, not around here."

"I'm telling you," said Jack, raising his voice as Indians seldom did and shaking his fist at the general, "this is your chance."

Then Hooker Jim interrupted the proceedings by getting up. He grabbed Meacham's coat and put it on and said, "Me Meacham now. Me make promise strong."

Meacham, eager to ease the tension, played along with Hooker Jim and offered him his hat and said, "Here, Jim, take my hat and put it on, then you will be Meacham."

"I'll get your hat pretty darn quick, no hurry. Soon enough it will be mine."

Winema and Meacham exchanged worried glances. Then Captain Jack said. "What do you say, General? Do you agree?" He waited a moment, and then continued, "Tell me. I'm tired of waiting for you to speak."

Abe sensed that something was wrong. Both Hooker Jim and Slolux were moving. "Answer him, General," Abe urged. "Tell him what Meacham was saying about a place in Big Valley?"

"Miller, I told you to keep your mouth shut," Canby ordered angrily.

"General!" Meacham's voice betrayed panic. "For heaven's sake, can't we promise him something?"

Captain Jack got up and walked away as though he had given up on the negotiations.

Meacham called to him. "Jack, come back. Listen, I will ask the Great Father in Washington for you people. We'll work out something."

Jack wheeled and marched up to the seated general. "You could do it today, if you would," he accused. Then in Modoc he shouted, *"Ut wih kutt,"* as he pulled a pistol and pointed it at the general.

Winema screamed; her husband, Frank Riddle, yelled, "Run! Run for your lives!" as he jumped up and took off.

The cap snapped on Jack's pistol, but it misfired. He drew back the hammer again as the general was rising to his feet. The Indian pulled the trigger again. This time it fired, and the ball struck the general below the right eye. Shocked, Abe reached out to steady the general and help him stagger away, but they had gone no more than a few feet when Bogus Charley tripped the general and jumped on him. Before Abe could do a thing, the Indian had slit the general's throat.

In all the frenzy, Abe was aware of other guns firing all around him as the peace commissioners tried to run for cover. Seeing there was no hope for the general, Abe, too, took off running toward the army camp.

As he stumbled over the rocky ground, he was aware of others running near him—Winema, Leroy Dyar—and up ahead was the form of Frank Riddle. A great uproar had commenced among the soldiers as they scrambled for their guns or ran for their horses. Even before Abe and the others got to their lines, the troops mounted a charge toward the peace council tent.

As Abe merged with the soldiers, he looked back in time to see the Modocs scrambling to safety in their lava bed stronghold. In a semi-trance, he jogged back toward the council site along with the converging soldiers.

He pushed through the milling soldiers, as the officers shouted orders. There on the ground lay General Canby—dead. Nearby . . . Reverend Thomas—dead.

And lying where he had fallen, Alfred Meacham, severely wounded and half scalped.

Chapter 25

It took three days after the peace council ambush before the army rallied to attack the Modocs' Lava Bed stronghold. In spite of the army's overpowering numbers, the attack was futile. The Modoc chief had planned his defenses well, and at first only soldiers died. Even the mortar shells did no critical damage until one fell without detonating. Then, when a couple Indians tried to open it with an axe, it exploded, killing them both. Otherwise, the army had no confirmed enemy killed.

On April 17, the army finally managed to rush the stronghold . . . only to find that Captain Jack and his men had withdrawn deeper into the Lava Beds during the night.

By then, Meacham had made a remarkable recovery in spite of his grave injuries. What the army doctors couldn't do for him, Winema's dedicated nursing had accomplished, and the man was up and walking around the camp. When he decided to go home to his family in Salem, Oregon, Abe Miller offered to accompany him as far as Linkville.

Abe was confused and angry. He needed to talk to Davis or Mary about what had happened. Everything had gone so very, very wrong. He had stayed at the army camp hoping to make some sense out of the tragedy. He wasn't sure what he expected . . . maybe someone saying that it wasn't really his fault . . . but that hadn't happened, and Abe felt more and more guilty about the deaths of Canby and Thomas. But he was angry, too. He had trusted Captain Jack, had gone out on a limb for him, and the Modoc chief had betrayed him.

The ride to Linkville was a silent one. Abe didn't feel comfortable talking to Meacham yet; he didn't know how the
Indian agent felt about what had happened. When they finally
arrived in Linkville, Abe went at once to the bank where Mary
was working. She agreed to have lunch with him, but during
their meal, she made it clear that she didn't appreciate or
understand what Abe had done. "Yes, it was a mistake, a big
mistake, Abe," she said cooly. "My father may not have the
best of motives in his heart, but he sure knew what he was
talking about when he warned that the Modocs intended to
murder General Canby."

Davis wasn't much comfort to him, either. "Let's clear out of
here," his friend said. "I think we belong back East."

It was tempting. Abe had had enough of Indian wars or
Indian anything, for that matter. But something held him. "I
can't," he finally said to his friend. "I've got to see this thing
through."

"See it through? What's that mean? Are you going to keep on
trying to force a peace that doesn't exist? When you make a
mistake, you've got to admit you were wrong. You can't just
keep stirring the same old pot to make amends. Look," Davis
said, jabbing a finger at Abe, "you're not very well liked around
here, you know. There's talk. People know what happened.
And you have to admit . . ." He stopped, seeing the hurt look in
Abe's eyes. "Well, I mean, in discrediting Bauder's warning,
you heaped a lot more fuel on the fire."

Abe knew that was true. On the other hand, he had only
been standing up for what he thought was right. It was all so
confusing. Why had everything backfired. Why?

Abe thought about Davis's suggestion for a long time. "You
might be right that going back east would be best, but . . . I
can't do it. I'm gonna go back down there to that army camp."

• • •

It took another week before scouts located the Modocs'

new camp, four miles deep in the Lava Beds.

Two weeks after the shooting of Canby, Thomas, and Meacham, a reinforced reconnaissance patrol headed out from Gillem's Camp on a beautiful spring morning. With a total of seventy-nine men, Captain Evan Thomas was feeling confident. Before the day was out, he would secure Hardin Butte so General Gillem could move his mortars closer and have a greater impact on the Modoc's new stronghold.

The patrol included Lieutenant Wright—who by then had a good deal of the cockiness kicked out of him—fourteen Warm Springs Indians—acting as scouts and traders—and two civilians. Reno Bauder was along as guide; he knew the area as well as anyone. And Abe Miller had volunteered to pack Doctor Bernard Semig's surgical supplies and help as a medic . . . if needed. Given his confusion about his responsibility for the deaths of Canby and Thomas, it seemed the least he could do.

Bauder ignored Abe for most of the morning as the column of twos snaked its way over the rough, flat land south of the camp. The rancher from Lost River rode beside Captain Thomas at the front of the column. He and the captain were the only two men on horseback. Lieutenant Wright marched in front of them. Still further forward, about twenty men from E Company were deployed in a ragged line of skirmishers.

Abe's pack was heavier than he had anticipated. He carried no gun or ammunition, but along with the doctor's equipment and the stretcher, he had to pack his own rations, blanket, slicker, and water—just like the rest of the soldiers.

I do feel a little bit like a soldier, he thought as he swung along. They were marching at ease, but he noticed that he was staying in step with the trooper on his right. How easy it would be to join up. Most of the soldiers were decent sorts. They hated this war just as much as he did, and now he was marching beside them. His pants were old army pants. All he'd have to do would be to trade in his black hat for a blue cap, and pick up an army jacket. I bet I can shoot better than a lot of these guys, Abe thought. I never used to miss a squirrel in the oak grove back home. The guy next to him had grown up in San Francisco and joined the army two months earlier to get away from the smell of the waterfront. With the minimal training the army gave, what good could he be, Abe thought, even with his new Spencer carbine?

Crazy thoughts . . . Abe shook his head and took a long drink from his canteen. His thoughts had taken a strange turn.

By about eleven o'clock, the patrol was moving in a south-easterly direction. Lava flows of a rougher, newer sort paralleled their march about a hundred yards distance on each side. Their craggy bluffs rose steeply thirty to forty feet above the flatter bottom land, and it was hard for the vanguard of skirmishers to climb them. Soon, the men drifted lower and lower until they were grouped on the floor of the valley out in front of the main column of men. No one was on top of the ridges to give an early warning if the Indians were near.

Even the column was getting sloppy as the men broke ranks to talk in groups of threes and fours. Doctor Semig was very concerned about this carelessness, and Abe heard one of the officers complain to a sergeant, but the corrections were half-hearted, and soon the troops were bunching up again. Abe tried to avoid this laziness and march where he was supposed to. He wasn't going to shoot a gun, but at least he could behave like a good soldier.

Abe was watching the guidon wave in the soft, morning breeze at the front of the column when he saw Bauder pull out and head his mount back down the line. Oh no, thought Abe. Here comes trouble. The horse was a powerful, prancing bay. Bauder sidled up to Abe and caused the shoulder of the horse to bump into him. Under his heavy load, Abe lost his balance and stumbled into the soldier on his left.

"Come on, Miller," the soldier said. "Look where you're going."

"Sorry," Abe said. "It wasn't my fault. Bauder here can't control his mount."

"Now isn't that too bad," Bauder mocked, turning his horse and riding alongside. "Didn't know your legs were so rubbery that a little brush would knock you down. But then I should've noticed that you're all tuckered out."

Abe didn't say a thing; just kept walking.

"You like this soldiering?" Bauder taunted.

"I ain't soldiering."

"Why . . . so you're not. Don't have a gun or nothing. Well, you just keep totin' those litter poles, and pretty soon you'll be strong enough to carry a rifle."

"I don't intend to carry a rifle," Abe shot back, looking up at the big man who was riding slightly ahead of him. The bright sun was over Bauder's shoulder, and it made Abe squint.

"Well, what are you doing out here? You're not harrassin' these good men, are you?"

"I came along to help Doctor Semig."

"No, you didn't," Bauder sneered. "You came along because you're feeling guilty . . . guilty about Canby and Thomas—good men you killed by your cowardly, infernal meddling."

Abe walked in silence, remembering what Davis had said. Was he trying to make amends? He had never intended to get involved with the war. But here he was, marching with a column of troops.

Bauder's loud voice shook Abe out of his reverie. "You all know who this is, don't you?" he jeered to everyone within earshot. "This here is Yellowbelly Miller . . . the guy who convinced General Canby to walk into an ambush."

Everyone knew that Abe opposed the war, and some knew he had urged Canby to go through with the parley. There were murmurs of agreement from several soldiers.

"He wants to protect those Indians so badly," Bauder went on, "that it wouldn't surprise me if he had a hand in settin' up the ambush. He's about as dumb as an Indian . . . probably thought that without Canby, the whole army would go home."

"You know that ain't so," Abe said in a measured voice. He clutched for some retort that would put Bauder in his place, but nothing came.

"You better believe it ain't so," Bauder said, intentionally misapplying Abe's words. "This army's not goin' home 'til we've exterminated every Modoc in the area. That right, boys?" There was a lame cheer.

"Well," said Abe, with all the determination he could muster, "I still hope this problem can be settled without any more bloodshed."

"Yeah, well, then maybe you're out here to warn the Indians that we're coming. But it won't work. I wager there'll be shootin' before this patrol's over. Then what'll you do, Miller? Run or fight?"

"I won't be running and I won't be fightin'," Abe said as he trudged along, keeping his eyes on the back of the man in front of him.

"Well, I'll put money on you runnin' 'cause down deep, you're yellow and soft as butter. You'll just hightail it back to camp. Yeah, Yellowbelly," Bauder drawled, "I bet that's just what you'll do. You don't belong out here with real men, anyway." He roared with laughter as he spurred his horse and headed back up to the front of the column. Some other men joined in the laughing.

Abe cringed. Something in Bauder's laugh told him that Bauder wasn't worried anymore that Abe might ruin his plans. To Bauder, Abe was a no-account. The war would go on in spite of Abe's efforts, and Bauder knew it.

They were coming into a basin area, surrounded on three sides. The lava bluffs, sometimes called Black Ledge, were close in to the right and left. And rising a hundred feet or so above them was Hardin Butte, directly to the front. This sandy hill closed off the end of the valley. Scattered around on the floor of the basin—like a bag of toy blocks that a child had dumped out—were scores of huge boulders, some the size of a man's pack and some as big as a horse. Meandering among them was a dry wash about four feet deep. Waters from the occasional torrential rains had roared through it, scouring out the ditch.

"Company . . . halt!" shouted the sergeant near the front. "All right, gentleman. This is where we're headed, so everybody take a break, and after a while we'll head on up this hill and reconnoiter a nest for them mortars."

The men broke out of what little formation they had maintained and strolled down to the bottom of the basin where some green grass grew among the sagebrush. They dropped to the ground casually to rest. Some got out their lunch; some took off their boots and rubbed their feet. No one bothered to put out guards or check the high ground. The Modocs were hidden away deep in the Lava Beds, after all.

Abe found a large rock away from the rest of the men and slid down behind it. It was his feud with Bauder that had left Abe weak-kneed, not the march. Abe shrugged out of his pack, and took a long draw from his canteen. What was he doing out here? He had come to Oregon, thinking the information he possessed would put right a great injustice and end this terrible war. But every time he turned around, it got worse . . . and now he'd had another row with Bauder.

He reached in his pack and pulled out a hunk of hardtack. He was knocking it on the rock to get the weevils out when, suddenly, the day exploded in violence. From every side of the lava rim, rifle fire rained down on the soldiers picnicking in the grassy bowl below. But other than little puffs of smoke from the crevices, there wasn't an Indian in sight.

Chapter 26

*T*he soldiers scrambled for cover in every direction, but they no sooner hunkered down behind one boulder to avoid fire from their front when they received crossfire from their rear. At first, they popped away valiantly at the most likely hiding places on the ridges, but it was useless. They had no real targets.

Abe lay plastered to the ground, a boulder on one side and sagebrush on the other. This is it, he thought. He had often wondered how he would react in a battle. It wasn't as though he had never faced danger before, but there was something very different about the merciless nature of all-out combat.

He could see a hundred yards or so across the basin, right to the base of Hardin Butte where Captain Thomas and Bauder had left their horses. The captain's horse had spooked and was running wildly back and forth. Bauder's horse was equally upset, rearing and pulling at the bush to which it was tied. Abe started to turn away, then saw Bauder's horse get hit and go down. Across all the noise of the battle he could hear it squeal in pain. Why should an innocent horse have to pay for this craziness? he wondered . . . and he remembered his prize mare and all the other horses that had died in the tornado back home.

Then a dozen men ran past Abe like a herd of mule deer, stooping low. Several had no guns, and a few were without boots. At first Abe thought one of them tripped, but then he realized that the man had taken a shot in the back. No one broke stride to give him a hand. The other men jumped into the gully and were gone, out of the trap.

Abe scooted forward to see the man who had been wounded. He was lying in the open, clawing for cover. Abe slithered toward him as fast as he could and got a hold on the man's shirt collar and one suspender. Pulling with all his strength, he soon had the man behind the bushes. But it was too late . . . the man was dead.

Abe recoiled from the body in horror. Had he been too rough in pulling the man to cover? Maybe he should have gotten Doctor Semig. Abe knew the dead man slightly. He'd been a hardluck gold miner before he joined the army. Said he had a wife and three kids and always talked about how he was going to bring them up from Shasta City as soon as the weather was good enough. Well, it was spring, and the weather had broken. Abe wondered if they were on their way . . . a fine reunion they'd have now. He reached out and touched the body.

Except for scalping, the Modocs did not mutilate the bodies of their enemies, but they would strip them of valuables. Abe reached in the man's pockets. There was an old watch with all the engraving worn smooth, a couple coins, and a wallet with a picture of a very beautiful woman. The picture showed a lot of resemblance to the man, and Abe wondered if it was a picture of his mother rather than his wife. He stuffed everything in his pack and backed away, almost unable to take his eyes off the body. He kept hoping it would show some signs of life . . .

One by one other men slipped past. Their eyes were wide; some had minor wounds. Cowards, thought Abe. They're fleeing under fire. But then, who was he to call anyone a coward? He wasn't fighting.

Dust and smoke from the guns filled the air. Somewhere, Abe could hear an officer trying to yell commands. The bugle was sounding, but in the middle of its call, the notes pinched off in a funny squeak.

Abe decided that if he was going to be any help as a medic,

he'd better find Doctor Semig who was probably toward the center of the action. He crawled over to the dry wash, and slipped down into it. Two more men went by him——running north, out of the fire. But Abe moved south, up the gully toward Hardin Butte and the heavier action. He crept along until he came to a man who was groping blindly.

"I dunno what happened," the soldier said as Abe came to his side. "Guess my old buffalo gun blew up in my face . . . I can't see a thing." There was indeed an ugly powder burn from his nose up. It was bluish black, except where some angry red blisters were forming. The blast had singed off his eyebrows and lashes, and the front part of his hair not covered by his cap was burned to curly-ended stubble. Abe poured some water from his canteen into the man's eyes and then made him as comfortable as possible in the bottom of the wash.

Abe was closer to the main body of soldiers now and heard Captain Thomas call out, "Men, we're surrounded. Wright, take your men, and see if you can work your way back over to the west end of that south ridge. We've got to secure it, or we'll be completely trapped in here. Cranston, take five men and see if you can clear those rocks up there to the northeast. Make sure you keep that north valley open for us. Now, where is everybody else?"

Abe watched as both groups of men moved out. Then he crawled out of the wash toward Thomas and his men. A bullet hit near his foot and sprayed it with a wave of sand. He rolled quickly back against a boulder as a jolt of fear went through him. That was close! he thought. I could be without a foot right now. I'd better slow down and be more careful. He was trembling all over. Here I am in the middle of a battle . . . and not doing anyone any good. It's one thing to die doing something useful, but I don't want to be shot like a lizard scampering across a rock.

He lay there a few more minutes, then eased out to work his

way over the sharp lava and between the dry sage.

When Abe found Doctor Semig, the doctor was doing his best to stop the bleeding in the neck of a young soldier who looked no older than sixteen. Abe noticed that blood had soaked the doctor's knee. He told the doctor about the dry wash and suggested that they move any wounded men there for better cover. The doctor agreed, provided the wounded were so seriously injured that they couldn't shoot. "I've been in enough firefights to know that we're in a heap of trouble. We need every gun we can get. Here, you drag this guy back to the wash. Just keep this pad on his neck."

Back in the gully as Abe worked on him, the kid came to. "I ain't . . . gonna . . . make it, . . . am I?" He gasped for breath between words and gripped Abe's arm so hard that he thought the boy's fingers would surely puncture his skin. There was a gurgling sound coming from the kid's throat.

"You're gonna be okay . . . here, lean back against the bank. Now, hang on . . . you'll be all right." But Abe didn't believe a word he had said. The guy looked like he'd die any minute.

"I'm not going . . . to live. Pray . . ."

"Now you shut up. You're gonna be okay."

"You . . . tell 'em . . . I didn't run." And then he passed out.

Abe tied a rag to hold the pad to the boy's neck, then turned as he heard someone coming. It was Bauder running full speed across a small opening toward the gully. As he turned his head to look back the way he'd come, he stumbled off the bank. He hit the stream bed below with one leg that collapsed under him as he tumbled head over heels, and rolled over sideways twice more.

For a moment Bauder lay still in the cloud of dust. But when he tried to rise, a great bellow erupted from him, and he fell back on the ground, cursing sharply through his teeth. "Useless leg!"

"Where you goin' so fast, Bauder?" Abe said.

"What the . . . Yellowbelly, what you doin' down in this hole?"

"It ain't no hole, Bauder. It's a wash, and I'm tendin' the wounded. Looks like you just brought me some more work."

Bauder looked up and down the wash, then back to Abe. "This wash, it goes all the way back, doesn't it? I remember ridin' past it. It's a way out of here, ain't it?"

"I've seen a few go by." Abe was still trying to adjust the soldier with the neck wound so each breath didn't make that haunting gurgle.

"Come here and see if you're smart enough to do anything for my leg," Bauder barked. Abe crawled over to him, keeping his head down. There was no doubt that he had broken his leg. Abe had set bones for animals before but never for a man. Still, he found a couple of stout sticks and whittled off their ends and rough spots. Then, with his own belt, Bauder's belt, and a few bandages, he rigged a splint.

While Abe worked, no "please" or "thank you" came out of Bauder's mouth, only a groan or curse now and then when Abe moved his leg. Frankly, Abe didn't much care whether Bauder ever walked again or not.

The rapid rifle cracks that had been occurring since the beginning of the surprise attack seemed to slow. "Maybe it's about over," Abe said hopefully.

"Over? Not unless all of Thomas' men are dead," Bauder groaned.

"Well, maybe the Modocs have pulled back."

"Miller, you don't know nothin', do ya? If those Indians are movin' at all, they won't be pullin' back; they're probably sneakin' down here to finish us off."

Abe tied the last knot on the splint and went back over to the soldier with the neck wound. The boy had slid down the bank and was gurgling again.

"Forget him," Bauder muttered. "Come here and give me a hand. Let's get out of here while we can."

"Not while I got more wounded to tend."

"I said, come over here! Even this escape route down the

gully's liable to be cut off pretty soon."

Abe's back was to Bauder as he continued to work.

"Miller, listen to me. As far as I'm concerned, your life ain't worth nothin' if you won't help me. Now get over here."

Abe didn't turn.

"Yellowbelly, I ain't messin' with ya no more."

Abe heard a click and was realizing that it sounded like a hammer being cocked when there was a bang behind him and a slug slammed into the bank not a foot away. He wheeled around to see Bauder holding a double-barreled derringer on him.

"I said we're gettin' out, Yellowbelly. Either you help me now, or you can be mighty sure you won't see the light of another day. That flatlander, Thomas, doesn't know a thing 'bout fightin' Indians, and I sure ain't gonna pay for his foolishness. With a busted leg, I ain't got a chance come dark. So you're gonna help me."

Abe looked at him for a long moment. "You're right, Bauder. You don't have a chance on your own. But I sure ain't gonna cut and run to save your skin. Your only hope is to stay put with the rest of us." Abe turned his back on the giant and crawled across the wash to climb the side and go aid other wounded men.

"Yellowbelly!" Bauder bellowed a string of vile curses and fired again.

The shot hit Abe in the left shoulder hard enough to cause him to spin and slide back down the small bank. He looked at his shoulder. It didn't feel like the slug had struck bone, but the blood was already spreading down to his elbow. That guy's a maniac, thought Abe. He meant to kill me. I ought to rip that splint right off his leg. Instead, Abe crawled back to the medic pack and got a bandage. He knew the derringer was empty, but this time Abe didn't turn his back on Bauder.

The pain was starting. It was a heavy ache, and at first he thought it wasn't going to be too bad. But then it got worse, pressing in, harder and deeper, demanding all his attention, closing out everything else, making his world go dark. Just this arm . . . can't get a breath . . . going to pass out . . . it's dark around the edges. Hang on, hang on . . . Take deep, steady breaths. Watch the sand . . . don't let it disappear. There, there . . . now it's steady. Push back the black. The light is growing.

Abe took several deep breaths, began to wrap the bandage around his shoulder.

"Hey, Miller, where you been? I need my supplies. Get 'em up here." It was Doctor Semig calling from a nearby rock pile. Suddenly the rifle fire picked up again with a vengeance. "Oh . . . took one in the shoulder, did you?" the doctor noted.

Abe looked over at Bauder but didn't say anything.

"Bring that stuff over here, and I'll wrap you up," Semig said. "I can't move around much with this knee."

Abe picked up the pack with his good arm and scrambled up out of the gully and over to the doctor. He lay on the ground behind some boulders as the doctor, hunching low, wrapped his shoulder tightly.

The bleeding slowed. Abe could still use his hand some, but the wound restricted his movement, and the pain wasn't much better.

"Listen," said Semig, "I've got two men right over yonder. I want you to get them down there in the wash where they'll be a little safer." Then he turned and was gone.

Abe stayed put. It was already the middle of the afternoon. How much longer was this going to continue? When he'd heard men talk about other Indian fights, they always reported them as short, hit-and-run affairs. But this was more like a battle out of the Great War. Abe realized that some of these men had fought in that war between the states . . . Captain Thomas, for instance. He was the son of Brigadier General Lorenzo Thomas, Abe recalled. And the other officers, each of them had military fathers. It must run in their blood, this thirst for violence. Abe despised them for it.

But he had a job to do. Abe moved out and found the men Doctor Semig had mentioned. One was gut shot and in so much pain that he was delirious, calling Abe "mother" and asking for water. It took Abe a long time to get him back to the wash and settled.

When Abe finally made the trip for the second man, storm clouds had begun to fill the sky. He still hadn't seen even one Indian. As he crawled along, he caught glimpses of the ridge that Cranston and his men had tried to take. To his horror, he could actually see the bodies of four soldiers lying in the open on the slight incline at the base of the bluff. Two looked like heaps of dirty laundry thrown on the ground. Another was lying spread-eagle on the top of a boulder. It looked like he had fallen there from above. The fourth was just below him.

Counting Cranston, there had been a total of six. Abe could see the bodies of four . . . no more than two could have made it to the top.

Abe looked over to where the captain and his men had dug in. They were still fighting hard. From time to time the Indians lobbed stones down onto their position. Apparently, the soldiers had barricaded themselves behind the rocks so well, that the Indians couldn't get a straight shot. Maybe the Modocs hoped that if someone jumped after being hit by a stone, he would provide a better target.

Abe went on to get the second man. This one had a head wound and the doctor had bandaged him so his eyes were covered. But the soldier was coherent and able to move under his own strength with Abe's guidance.

"Where we goin'?" the soldier asked.

"Over to a gully where you'll have better cover," Abe said.

"Well then, I'm takin' my Sharps. I got it loaded with a charge of double-aught. With all these savages around, I ain't gonna be without it." But as they started to crawl, the rifle got caught in the brush and dug into the sand. The soldier made very little headway carrying the big weapon.

Finally Abe said, "Here, let me carry that. You're just getting it full of sand anyway." Abe noticed that the hammer was cocked.

They slid into the gully a short distance from their destination. Some brush on the bank of the old creek bed hid the make-shift infirmary. When Abe crawled around the corner, he saw his first Indian of the battle . . . looking right at him.

Time slowed, and the scene seemed to freeze like a painting in which Abe noticed every detail. The Indian was kneeling; under him, Bauder lay on his belly in the dirt. The Indian had a knee right between Bauder's shoulder blades and with one handful of Bauder's hair was pulling his head back at an unbelievable angle. In the Indian's other hand was a big skinning knife, poised to take Bauder's scalp. A grimace of extreme pain was on Bauder's face, and it looked like he was screaming.

But all Abe heard was an ear-splitting blast. The Indian's head snapped back, his face exploding in a crimson star burst. Both arms went out like a man on a cross as he flew up in the air and landed once, then bounced another two feet on the hard creek bottom.

Abe whipped around to see who had fired the shot and only then realized that the Sharps in his hand had a hot barrel. His finger was still on the trigger.

Chapter 27

"What happened? What happened?" begged the bandaged soldier behind Abe.

"Hey, Yellowbelly," Bauder gasped as he rolled over and sat up. "I can't believe it. I can't believe it! You got some sand in you after all." And he broke into a high, hysterical laugh.

"Shut up," snapped Abe as he threw the rifle aside. He turned and grabbed the shirt of the soldier behind him and roughly pulled him along to where the other wounded men lay. Then he went on up the wash a short way and vomited once, twice, and then it was the dry heaves.

For the next hour, Abe moved in a fog. He brought more men from Captain Thomas' holdout back to the safety of the gully. He learned that, not only had Cranston's detail been wiped out, but Wright and his men had been slain too. Not knowing this, Thomas had tried to hail him, only to be answered by a volley of bullets from the very ridge that Wright was supposed to secure.

But to Abe, nothing mattered. He moved like a walking dead man, numbly going here and there, doing what he was told. Once his hat got shot off as he crawled across an open space. He stood straight up and walked over, picked it up, and put it on without getting hit. All he could think of was the exploding face of the Indian floating before his eyes. Over and over little pieces of red and white and yellow sprayed out into the air, and the gun in his hand was hot. "I couldn't have done it . . . it must have been an accident . . . I didn't do it," he murmured to himself. But he knew he had.

The scene that moved so slowly and vividly in his mind began to include his bringing up the Sharps, sighting with the skill he'd learned in hunting squirrels, and pulling the trigger. He couldn't believe that he had done it; but he had, and as time passed, he remembered every minute movement of the deed.

Back in the ditch, Abe held the kid with the neck wound as he died. His last wheezy words were, "Please . . . pray."

Abe knew the boy deserved more, but all he could think of was, "God be merciful to me a sinner." He said it over and over as he rocked back and forth with the boy's head in his lap. He knew it was a verse from the Bible, but try as he might, he couldn't remember who had said it. It just seemed right.

Suddenly, a dozen of the men who had been fighting alongside Thomas dropped back to the dry wash. Several were wounded. Doctor Semig was with them, but he had taken another hit, this one in the shoulder. His strength was giving out. "Miller," he said. "Go back and see if you can find Thomas and the other two."

There was a lull in the shooting. Dark clouds that had been spreading across the sky swallowed the sun, though it was still two fingers above the horizon. The basin floor became cold and dreary as Abe crawled between the sagebrush and boulders. He came to the holdout. The men had created a makeshift fort by piling stones between the larger boulders. There, Abe found Captain Thomas. Two of his men were sprawled on the ground. From their contorted positions, Abe knew they were dead without checking them.

As Abe slipped into the enclosure, he whispered softly, "Captain Thomas . . . Captain Thomas. It's me, Miller." Abe crept over to him. The captain was drawing a careful bead on something up on the south ridge. The ridge was still in sunlight, and Abe tried to see what he was aiming at. Then he saw it—a brief movement between some rocks. Then it became clearer: an Indian, sitting right there, not more than seventy-five yards away. Abe watched, almost flinching as he waited for the captain's rifle to go off. But nothing happened.

"Hey," whispered Abe to the captain. "That's Scarfaced Charley. I recognize his shirt." The Modoc shifted farther into the open, but the captain didn't fire. "What's the matter?" Abe said as he crawled up beside the officer. Then he saw that the captain was dead, shot right through the forehead. He'd been dead before Abe ever got there.

The horror of talking to a dead man as though he were alive caused Abe to go dizzy. Nothing was real anymore. He pulled away to the other side of the small circle. The guns were finally quiet, and he felt alone. Wind off the lake five miles to the north was blowing hard and cold, and the dark clouds were churning above him. He'd come a long way from his happy, childhood home in Goshen. He'd ventured far beyond Kansas . . . beyond civilization . . . beyond the protection of the army. Now he sat in a circle of stones in a worthless volcanic wasteland. No wonder the area was called the "Devil's Homestead." Three corpses were his only companions. Even the spilt blood had turned cold and hard. But for what? For what?

Abe had started this journey west trying to get away from the painful memories of his deceased family. And then, angry at God for the senseless death and violence in the world, he had set out to stop it. Bauder and Mary on the train, the robber in Kansas, the Modoc War—his efforts had been inept at best, and fatally mistaken at worst . . . total failures. A storm of violence had followed him wherever he went. And now he was a part of it . . . more than part of it, a participant, a killer himself.

"I'm no different than the others," he murmured to himself. "I'm really no different . . ." He took a deep breath and let it slide out. It's true, he thought. But as awful as it sounded, he somehow felt better for admitting it.

Abe rolled over and stared up at the sky. Another shot rang out, its crack cut short by the wind. Abe flinched. There'd been so much blood, so much death . . . couldn't it stop?

He looked up at the ridge again. Scarfaced Charley had pulled back behind the rocks, but Abe could still see a corner of his shirt. Suddenly, Abe slipped up and over the makeshift bulwark. He crawled fast through the brush and boulders. His shoulder was burning with new pain, and he could feel fresh wetness on his chest. But he went on. The ground sloped more steeply up to Scarfaced Charley's position. He inched his way closer, from bush to rock to bush.

From above him, a shot rang out. The bullet hit within inches of Abe's head, showering it with stinging rock fragments. "Don't shoot! Don't shoot, Charley!"

"If I'd meant to kill you, I could have . . . several times today. Why do you come up here, Crazy Abe? You should be home."

"I came," Abe said, wheezing great gulps of air as he came closer. "I came to ask you to stop."

"To stop?"

"Yeah. To cease fire. To withdraw."

"Why should I do that?"

"Isn't it obvious?" Abe said, craning his neck to see the Indian tucked behind the rocks of the ridge. "There's been so much killing today. Certainly you don't want all your men wiped out?"

Scarfaced Charley laughed quietly. "No. I wouldn't want that. Do you think my men might be wiped out?"

"We've lost scores. There's only . . . there's less than twenty soldiers left, and some of them are so badly wounded that they won't last the night."

"Plenty more ran back to Gillem's camp. Why didn't you run, Crazy Abe?"

Abe ignored the question. "I bet there's at least twenty-five bodies down there, dead on the field. And that's just army dead. Add to those all the Modoc dead, and certainly this day has been too bloody. Why don't you call it off?"

Scarfaced Charley was silent for a minute. "Yes. That would make twenty-six . . . a great coup."

"You lost twenty-six? See what I mean?" said Abe. "That's about the same as the army. Isn't that enough?"

Scarfaced Charley grinned wryly. "No, Crazy Abe. I only started with twenty-two braves. Little Ike has not come back. So now I have twenty-one men."

The meaning of Scarfaced Charley's statement took a while to sink in. Then it hit Abe with a shock: a mere twenty-two Indians had routed the whole patrol of seventy-nine troops. And the Modocs had sustained only one casualty . . . That one casualty must have been the Indian I shot, thought Abe, the one trying to scalp Bauder.

"You lost only one man?" Abe said weakly. "I don't believe you. Surely you've lost more than that."

"I not lie," the Modoc said with a resolute shake of his head.

"If it's like you say, then why would you want to kill more soldiers? You've more than won."

Scarfaced Charley shrugged. "We've not won. It does no good to kill soldiers. The more we kill, the more come. I am tired of this blood."

"Then call off your men," Abe urged, "and go home."

"Can't leave."

"Why not?"

"Modocs never leave a brother on the battlefield. Little Ike is still down there. We fight 'til we can get him."

Abe thought for a moment. "I'll make a deal. I'll bring Little Ike to you, if you will leave."

Scarfaced Charley turned to look out over the basin. From time to time a rifle cracked in the stormy afternoon. "Deal," he said, turning back to Abe.

"Good. Tell your men to cease fire while I go after Little Ike."

Scarfaced Charley laughed. "Not a chance, Crazy Abe. We fight 'til you bring him up here."

"Come on," said Abe. "I'm liable to get shot."

"You came up here once; do it again," Scarfaced Charley

said with a shrug, moving off behind a nub of lava and out of Abe's sight.

Once back in the gully, Abe found the body of Little Ike. Someone had dragged it away from the wounded soldiers. It was hard to carry the Indian, and Abe was in such a hurry that he failed to tell the soldiers about his plan. By the time he realized his mistake, they, too, were shooting at his dark shape struggling across the basin and up to the south ridge. He made a good target for both the Indians and the soldiers. Twice before he got to the protection of the crevice, slugs made the corpse across his back jerk as they slammed into it.

When he got to where Scarfaced Charley had been, no one was there. "Charley," he called softly. "Charley, I brought Little Ike." But there was no response. He risked calling a little louder. Finally Abe gave up. He dropped the body like a sack of grain behind some rocks, and stumbled back toward the soldiers.

When he slipped back into the dry wash, drops of rain had started to fall. "Hold your fire! It's me," he called before he showed himself around the bend in the creek bed as he approached the others.

"'Me,' who?" someone challenged.

"Abraham Miller."

"They're comin'; they're comin' to get us," a panicky voice screamed.

"Maybe they are, but that ain't no Injun," The voice was Bauder's. "Come on in, Miller."

Then, from the top of the south ridge, a voice called out over the whole basin. "All you fellers that ain't dead yet had better go home. We want to save a few of you for another day."

In the silence that followed, a man began to cry. It was over . . . finally over. Abe felt like crying too. A great streak of lightning flashed and the rain came down, stinging and cold.

Chapter 28

*T*he little company of shot-up survivors made their way slowly back down the valley toward Gillem's camp. Some men crawled, while others supported one another as they staggered along the gully. Fortunately, they did not have far to go before reinforcements met them. With them came a detail of men, leading eleven donkeys outfitted with litters for carrying the wounded.

The most critical of the seventeen wounded men rode while Abe and the others had to walk through the driving rain which soon turned to sleet. It was nearly dark before they arrived at the warmth of the hospital tent.

Abe fell asleep moments after collapsing on a cot. Sometime in the night a doctor came and awoke him to examine his shoulder. Abe couldn't help groaning with pain when the doctor pulled the bandage away to clean the wound.

"I think this will heal nicely with nothing more than a few stitches," the doctor said as he held a lamp close. Then he frowned. "What were you shot with, anyway, son? This hole looks like it was made by a very small caliber bullet."

Abe just gritted his teeth as the doctor probed and cleaned the wound. He could still recall Bauder pointing that little derringer at him.

When the doctor finished suturing up the wound, he said, "You're lucky, young man. Many of the others didn't fair so well. We may still lose a couple more, and several have required amputations. Even Doctor Semig lost his leg. Now, why don't you get some sleep."

• • •

Jonathan Davis was sitting by Abe's cot when he awoke. Somehow his old bowler hat had been crushed. "Just can't keep out of this war, can you, ol' boy?" he grinned. "How are you feeling this morning?"

Abe sat up and tried moving his shoulder. It was stiff and it hurt—hurt a lot—but the pain was bearable. "I guess I'll make it," he said, but he couldn't return his friend's smile.

"Hold tight, and I'll be back in a flash," Davis said, hurrying out of the tent.

Abe swung his feet to the ground and tried pulling on his boots, but they were still wet and cold. He wrapped a blanket around himself and waited.

When Davis returned, he had two tin cups of steaming coffee. They sat on the cot and sipped the hot brew as Davis asked questions about what had happened the day before. He had obviously heard most the story already, including how Abe had saved Bauder's life, but when he asked how Abe got wounded, Abe just shrugged . . . and got a stab of pain in his shoulder for his efforts.

"Come on," said Davis, "you must know somethin'."

Finally Davis wormed it out of him.

"That makes it all the more remarkable that you saved Bauder's life," observed Davis.

"It's nothin' to be proud of," said Abe dejectedly.

"You mean because you killed that Modoc in the process?"

"Right . . . the only Modoc killed in the whole attack."

"But what else could you do? It was a natural reaction in a life and death situation. You can't punish yourself with guilt because you saved Bauder's life. It was one or the other."

"It was a 'reaction' made possible because I had a deadly weapon in my hand. If I hadn't been armed, I couldn't have killed anyone, now, could I?"

"True. But honestly, Abe . . . did you imagine that you could get so deeply involved in this war and keep your hands clean? I would have thought that the murder of General Canby and Reverend Thomas would have taught you a lesson."

Abe turned a pained look at his friend.

"Sorry, I didn't mean to bring that up again."

"No . . . it's okay. It just feels like I've taken a one-two punch. First, the fiasco at the peace council, then I shoot one of the Modocs I'm tryin' to protect." Abe looked away as he remembered the bloody battlefield. "Some kid out there wanted me to pray for him, and all I could say was, 'God be merciful to me a sinner.' I couldn't even remember where it came from."

"Sounds like a pretty good place to start when a person's feeling as low as you are."

"Didn't do any good. I don't think God hears me anymore. I've really messed things up. I feel guilty as sin."

Davis sat in silence for a while, then he said, "You ever pray the Lord's Prayer?"

"Sure. Why?"

"I seem to remember a line in there, something about, 'Forgive us our debts, as we forgive our debtors.'"

"So?"

"Could be you'll never feel free, never feel forgiven, as long as you can't forgive."

"Who, me? I don't hold nothin' against anyone."

"That ain't the way I hear it."

"Hear what?" Abe was feeling uncomfortable.

"Well, Bauder, for one. But even before you ever met him, you held a pretty big grudge against God for taking your family."

Abe thought about this as he sipped his coffee. "How could I forgive God? It's not like He sinned, or anything. He's . . . He's God. You know, perfect."

"I didn't say He did anything wrong. I only noted that you hold it against Him, like a debt. Maybe it's because you think He mismanaged your world that you feel like you have to run the rest of the world for Him. Maybe that's why you're obsessed with stopping this god-awful war single-handedly."

"Hey, didn't Jesus want us to be peacemakers?" Abe felt like kicking something. Why was Davis always sticking him with this line of talk?

"Sure, but you're no peacemaker, Abe. Look at you . . . and what's happened wherever you've stuck your nose. Make your peace with God . . . and forgive yourself. Then maybe He'll show you some small ways you can help others."

• • •

Ten days passed without one sighting of the Indians. People began to speculate that the Modocs had withdrawn from the entire region. And then on May 7, they attacked a supply train and administered another sound defeat to the army.

General Jefferson C. Davis, who had arrived to replace General Canby, ordered Captain Hasbrouck to take a contingent of men and go after the Modocs. Three days later Hasbrouck caught up with the Indians and, for the first time, got the better of them in a firefight . . . although only one Indian was killed.

After that, the tribe split and disbursed. Weeks passed as the army chased little bands of Modocs all over the country, capturing a few here and a few there.

Captain Jack was the last leading Modoc at large. And then on June 1, 1873, he surrendered of his own accord.

Two days later, Abe was at Fort Klamath where the Modocs were being held when a telegram arrived from General William T. Sherman, the commanding general of the whole United States Army. It instructed General Davis to dispose of the prisoners "according to law and justice, because that's what the press will be watching, but disperse the rest of the tribe in such a way that the name 'Modoc' will cease forever."

When the trial concluded, Captain Jack and three other

Modocs were found guilty of murdering General Canby and Reverend Thomas. As Abe was leaving the courtroom, Jonathan Davis caught up with him and said, "Well, I guess it's all over but the hanging. I've seen more of Oregon than I ever wanted to see. Now will you come back East with me? I gotta string some more barbwire."

"No, thanks," said Abe. "I think I'll stick around."

"Come on, Miller. You're not gonna try to stop that hangin' like you tried to stop the war, are you?"

Abe winced. "No. Nothing so dramatic as storming the gallows. I listened to what you said I've been trying to make my personal peace."

"Well then, what's keepin' ya here?"

"You heard the official order. General Sherman wants the name of 'Modoc' wiped off the face of the earth. I don't think that should happen. Wherever they send those Indians, I'm going with them."

"And do what?"

"I've been thinking about teaching school." He grinned at Davis. "Think that job's a little more my size?"

"You'd do a great job!" Davis slapped him on the shoulder; Abe flinched. "Oh. Sorry . . . Where are they sending them?"

"More than likely they'll ship them off to the Oklahoma Territory. I understand the Quakers run an Agency school for Indian children at a place called Quapaw. I'm thinking to volunteer."

"Well, I guess that ain't so far from Kansas, which is where you were headin' the first time I met you. But are you sure you want to go all the way down there by yourself?"

"No." Abe grinned. "Not by myself."

Davis studied him for a moment. "Now wait a minute! Wait just a flea-flickin' minute. You ain't ropin' me into goin' to the Territory. I'm heading back to civilization as fast as a train ticket can take me."

"I wasn't figurin' on asking you. I thought I'd speak to Mary

Bauder."

"What? You mean you and she . . . ?" Davis just stood there, first pointing to Abe and then back toward Linkville where Mary still worked in the bank. "I knew you were sweet on her . . . but you and Mary Bauder?"

"Sure. Why not? We've been talkin', and I think she understands me a little more now. And she's interested in teaching school, too. Anyway, I thought I'd at least ask."

Davis threw back his head and laughed, his bushy mustache spreading across his face. "Now that's the craziest idea you've had yet. But you're just fool enough to pull it off . . . this time."

Afterword

With the exception of Abe Miller, the Bauders, and Jonathan Davis, the main characters in this story are real and the historical events involving them are true.

While Reno Bauder is fictional, the ranchers along Lost River did play an active and possibly conspiratorial role in replacing A. B. Meacham, an Indian agent sympathetic to the Modocs, with T. B. Odeneal, whose hard-nosed policies favored the ranchers and the total removal of the Modocs from their homeland.

Those policies and various treacherous acts by the local ranchers led directly to the conflict known as the Modoc War, one of the most costly Indian wars on record, in which fifty-three poorly-armed Modoc warriors defended their ancestral home for six long months against more than a thousand soldiers.

After the war, the government allowed a few Modocs to return to the Klamath reservation, but it deported most of them to the Quapaw reservation in Oklahoma territory. There, they struggled for many years until Public Law 587, passed on August 13, 1954, terminated the federal government's recognition of the Modoc tribe.

However, in 1967 survivors reorganized a new tribal government. Eleven years later the federal government recognized Bill Follis as the first chief of the Modoc Nation since the death of Bogus Charley nearly a hundred years before. Today, the tribe lists about three hundred Modocs on its roll.

The name Modoc has not been wiped off the face of the

earth. It lives on in those descendants of the brave warriors of the Lava Beds, in the name of the northeastern-most county of California (the author's boyhood home), and in the hearts of all who mourn our nation's racist and unjust treatment of native American peoples.

About the Author

As a boy, Dave Jackson lived in "Modoc" country and even learned how to make arrowheads from a tribal member. Now he makes his home in Evanston, Illinois, where together with his wife Neta they have written over seventy-five books, including the popular Trailblazer series of award-winning historical fiction for young readers. He is currently working on a sequel to *Lost River Conspiracy*.